PALLADIUM'S FOLLY

JANET JOYCE HOLDEN

LLENNENDHRAD

PALLADIUM'S FOLLY

Janet Joyce Holden

Book Four in the Palladium Series

Janet Joyce Holden asserts the right to be identified as the author of this work.

This novella is a work of fiction. Names, characters, events portrayed are the work of the author's imagination. Any resemblance to actual persons, events or localities is coincidental.

Other books by this author -

The Origins of Blood vampire series –
BLOOD PATERNAL
BLOOD NOCTURNAL
BLOOD ETERNAL
BLOOD REVIVAL
BLOOD TERMINAL

The Carousel series –
CAROUSEL
THE ONLY RED IS BLOOD
DARK

The Palladium series –
PALLADIUM'S GATE
PALLADIUM'S FALL
PALLADIUM'S RISE
PALLADIUM'S FOLLY
PALLADIUM'S REDEMPTION

For the wild places.

1

ROGAN

It took him longer than expected to reach the Mission Inn at Riverside and consequently he was fifteen minutes late. Corinne Hill, his father's executive PA, was already seated at a table in the restaurant. She stood as he arrived, her eyebrows raised in consternation, her handshake almost as strong as Jake's.

"Sorry I'm late. The traffic."

"It took me a while to get here, too," she said, retaking her seat. "Didn't even see the coast as we were landing. This area is bigger than I thought." She stared at him across the table as he took the chair opposite, her severe expression underpinned by short, dark hair and a navy pant suit.

Having known her for years, he smiled at her scrutiny. "What?"

"Everything all right? You look to have lost a little weight."

"I'm fine."

She was about to reply when the waiter arrived.

"I guess Dad was too busy to come see me," he said, after they'd both ordered drinks.

"And I guess you couldn't take the time either, despite me sending you a first class ticket."

Rogan raised his hands in defeat. "How is he?"

"He tells me he's fine, same as you."

"Like father, like son, huh?"

"You have no idea how much." Corinne pushed a canvas duffle toward him. "Lap top, new phone, and a new black Amex card. I canceled the other after we saw multiple bills coming in from Vancouver."

He screwed his eyes shut for a moment and massaged his temples. His wallet had promptly vanished after he was kidnapped by Reave and the killer twins.

"Don't worry," she added. "I put in the paperwork for everything else that went missing."

"Thanks." He peered into the bag. "I don't suppose there's anything here on Stormquell?"

"Not sure. You'll have to take a look."

He nodded, watching her face, wondering how

much she'd been aware of over the years. Having helped keep him out of trouble on numerous occasions, she'd never asked any questions of her boss's lunatic son. Therefore, she took him by surprise when she said,

"So, how deep are you in?"

He reached into his jacket pocket, brought forth his emissary medal and slid it across the table. "Do you know what that is?"

For a long moment she stared at the shiny metal disk before reaching for it and turning it over in her fingers. "Christ."

"All this time, you knew—"

"Rogan—"

"No, really. Why did you all lie to me?"

In the poignant silence that followed, their drinks arrived. He wanted to hurl his glass across the room. Instead, he watched Corinne place the medal of office reverently on the table.

"Are we ready to order?" the waiter asked, cheerful and oblivious.

"I'll have the filet mignon, medium rare, and the loaded baked potato." Corinne raised a defiant eyebrow at Rogan.

"I'll have the same." He leaned back in his seat and got a grip on his temper. It was pointless yelling at Corinne. It wasn't her fault, but this whole business was making him feel like a little boy all over again.

"I'm sorry," she said when their server had gone. "I'd tell you your father thought it was for the best, but I realize how unsatisfactory that is." For a short while they sat in silence before she added, "Had you any inkling about the Rothe house before you arrived?"

"Nope. No dreams, visions, or premonitions. It was the resident ghost who pushed me in the right direction." He explained about Mr. Brown, the house's former caretaker.

"Of all the places. It's uncanny." Her fingers tapped the medal on the table. "As for this—"

"Am I the first?"

"I think so."

"I hear it's a great honor." Rogan collected the medal and slid it back into his pocket.

"Dr. Halberd told us about Jackal," she added. "What's he like?"

"Polite, formal, difficult, aggressive, singularly focused, and he has no idea what to make of me."

"I see, or maybe I don't."

"Jackal isn't our problem. Our problem is Draken, who's awakening to the idea of just how much he can accomplish here."

"Take over the world, you mean?"

"You can laugh. Have you met him?"

"No. Are we talking benevolent dictator or insane megalomaniac?"

He frowned. She wasn't taking him seriously. But then again, how could she? A year ago he wouldn't have believed any of this either, despite his enhanced perception. Except it was looking like she and his father knew about this stuff long before he did, grandly illustrated by her questions and the bag she'd pushed toward him without batting an eye, and the more he thought about it the more his anger grew at being kept in the dark.

Corinne clasped her hands on the table and watched him stew. "This reminds me of our last meeting," she said eventually. "The one where I told you not to go wandering off."

"Bet you never expected this, though?"

"No." She smiled.

Subsequent conversation limped along. Corinne wanted to make sure of his well-being at the Rothe house. Rogan offered her reassurances and held back about the little party tricks Jake had been teaching him, along with his newly-acquired fortitude. Both were relieved when the food arrived, allowing them to eat and drink in silence.

When they were done he gave her a ride back to Ontario airport in the old truck.

"We could get you a better vehicle—"

"This one is fine. What I want is access to everything you have on Palladium."

Corinne nodded. "I can't see your father objecting to that."

On arrival he hauled her carry-on bag from the back of the truck. They shook hands, said their goodbyes, and as soon as the departure hall doors swished shut, Gregory Brown, former caretaker of the Rothe house, materialized alongside him.

"So, they knew."

"Yep."

"And they never told you."

"Nope."

Climbing aboard the truck they rode in silence until, "What about your mother?" Brown asked eventually.

"What about her?"

"You never mention her."

"She died when I was a little boy." Rogan held up a hand. "And no, don't even *think* about going there."

"Sorry."

"It's okay."

Silence descended once more, but Rogan knew it wouldn't last. Thankfully, Brown's next subject was decidedly more bearable.

"The killer twins stole your wallet?"

"Seems like, and with any luck they left us a trail to follow."

"Not the best idea, chasing after them."

"No, but unless you have a better idea, they're the only link to Draken we've got."

It was a month since Reave's attack on the house

and thus far, neither he nor Brown had any idea where Draken had gotten to, or what had happened to Reave. At least it was quiet on the Palladium front. Rogan had yet to descend the ladder, and Jake had still to pay them a visit. Figuring out how Reave managed to build her monsters was obviously taking some time.

"What's the latest on the Italianate?"

His companion frowned. "Caroline Aldred is proving a hard nut to crack. Mary seems to think we'll need outside help."

"Esoteric or physical?"

"Esoteric for now. A lot depends on how much of a hurry we're in, wouldn't you say?"

Rogan shrugged. In all honesty he had no idea. Despite his all-business attitude with Corinne, the further they receded from that terrible day, the less he wanted to be involved in the aftermath. Was Reave dead or alive? Did he care? As for a dragon on the loose, the more he thought about it the more ridiculous it seemed.

It was dark by the time they arrived home.

"Maybe we should get together and come up with a plan. Tomorrow?"

Brown wrinkled his nose. "How about the day after tomorrow? I have a couple of meetings to attend."

Sure." Rogan jumped out of the truck and hauled open the gate. When he returned, the ghost of Gregory Brown was gone.

Despite his reluctance, he had to face facts and accept how much everything had changed. Everything. Even his status back home. No longer the crazy son of an east coast financier. Sitting opposite Corinne while she'd handed over the card, the laptop, not to mention the conversation they'd had regarding the house, and Jake, it was as if the doors had been thrown wide open. Welcome aboard, son, you're now part of the business.

But what kind of business, exactly? Questions about his dad swarmed around him like flies, especially after Reave had hinted his family knew more than they were letting on. About his mom, too, whom he barely remembered.

One bite at a time, the snake admonished, *otherwise, we'll choke.*

Dropping the bag on the table, he reached into his pocket, withdrew the medal of office and hung it inside the closet with his fancy jacket. For a moment he stared at the ensemble before closing the door. Something else he still had to reconcile, his new role as Palladium's Nembraean Emissary. Corinne's eyes had nearly popped out of her head when she saw the medallion, although she'd managed to cover up her astonishment very quickly.

Hungry, despite the restaurant dinner, he headed for the kitchen. There was no one around, the lights were off, but he discovered a wrapped sandwich in the refrigerator, left for him by Mrs. Harris, and he took it along with him as he strolled around the yard, still too restless to settle for the night.

A short while later, sandwich devoured, he arrived at the adjoining wall with the Italianate, specifically the section he and Mr. Grimes had hurried to rebuild some weeks ago. Already the honeysuckle was stretching forth, determined to reclaim the brickwork. He thought about the entity living over the other side of the wall and a smile appeared on his face. Brown was stalling, that much was obvious.

Oh, please don't do that, began the snake, as he placed one foot on the base of a brick pillar.

Climbing atop the wall he was able to see into the tangle of next door's yard, courtesy of a bright, rising moon. The house at its center was drowning in shadow, the surrounding undergrowth a choke of weeds, everything gasping for water and attention.

Movement below gave him a start and he almost fell back onto the Rothe house lawn. "Mrs. Aldred."

She had given him no warning of her approach. Her accompanying aura was a bitter miasma of rage and revulsion.

"I know why you're here," she said, as his fingers clawed frantically at the brickwork. She appeared carved of stone, her sickly face portrayed in unforgiving detail.

Cursing his recklessness, he sought a solution to his predicament. "Ma'am, I'm sorry to disturb you." He appraised the Italianate yard. "I was hoping we could engage in trade."

God, I hope you know what you're doing.

"Trade?" She was standing maybe five feet away. One step forward narrowed the distance to four. "What could you possibly possess that would be of interest to me?"

Rogan held up his hands. "These." He gestured toward her yard. "Maybe I could cut back some of this mess and give you something to look forward to when you step outside."

The apparition frowned for a moment. She seemed taken aback. Turning away she took a few steps toward the house and for a long moment stared into the tangle of vegetation. "You would do this for me?"

"Yes, ma'am."

"In exchange for what?"

"You already know the answer to that. I need to know about Reave."

"But it won't stop there, will it? Because it never does."

Think about your next words, warned the snake. *Think about them very carefully.*

Rogan took a deep breath. "Some of the other ghosts say you're a witch, and as we have a dragon on the loose, I thought maybe—"

"A dragon." In an instant she was directly in front of him, sunken eyes registering her fury. "On the loose. And whose fault is that?"

"Not yours, ma'am, but I was hoping you might have some advice."

Once again, she stepped away and he watched as she thought it over, all set to scramble down his side of the wall if she decided to murder him. Instead, she spun around and took in her yard once more, her substance so three-dimensional he heard the whisper of her petticoats as they swished through the tangle of weeds. Had he sold her on it?

She turned and offered him the faintest smile. "Make a start, and we'll talk." She set off toward the house and didn't look back.

What did we just do?

We just struck a bargain with a witch.

Like we don't have enough to worry about.

I'm not worried. We'll need her.

He climbed down and set off toward the cottage.

Not worried, my ass. You were scared shitless.

Rogan couldn't argue with that. He did, however, feel better for having gotten that particular confrontation over with, and once inside the cottage he left the deadbolts undone, got ready for bed and fell into a blissful sleep.

The following morning he sought out Dr. Halberd who was in his study, appraising a stack of mail.

"Young Master Renard is doing well in his studies." Halberd tapped the letter in his hand with a pudgy finger. "His father appears highly satisfied."

"That's good news," Rogan said, and having no other way to explain the bargain he'd struck with their ghostly neighbor, he simply came right out with it.

Halberd stared at him. "Really? How extraordinary."

"I'll make sure it's done in my spare time—"

The other man wasn't listening. Rising from the desk, he brandished his jailer's key ring and unlocked a nearby cupboard. "Extraordinary," he repeated, and began rummaging through the cupboard's contents. "We have an album of photographs in here, somewhere."

Rogan reached out and was soon holding an ever-growing stack of ledgers until, finally—

"Here we are." Halberd returned to the desk with a heavy album, its cover frayed with age, leaving Rogan staggering beneath a formidable pile of its companions.

After off-loading his burden onto a nearby chair he joined Halberd at the desk. "Wow, is that—?"

"All three houses? Yes, before the eucalyptus were planted. You see the dirt road? And yet we were still more civilized in those days than the communities further west."

"I don't see the gate."

"No, you wouldn't. The sigils were not employed until the nineteen twenties."

"Do we have anything specifically on the Italianate?"

"I'm hoping so. It would be helpful with your current endeavor, I should think."

Rogan nodded while basking in Halberd's enthusiasm. He hadn't thought about how his new pact would affect his job until this morning when a mild sense of panic had swept in. Thankfully, it didn't seem to be an issue.

With Halberd's blessing he took the album to the cottage and went through it, cover to cover. Not only did it contain photographs of all three houses, but their occupants, too, including an older man wearing a suit, a pocket watch, and a jaunty straw boater, accompanied by a much younger woman who appeared frail in her long dress and big fancy hat but nonetheless wore a smile on her face. He recognized her immediately, and a moment later he was smiling, too.

What a beauty, said the snake.

Rogan had to agree, and after a quick re-appraisal of the photos he grabbed a notebook. It was time to include the Italianate in Brown's already established collection of lists.

2

BROWN

The truth of the matter? Brown had given up on Caroline Aldred because he had no idea how to approach her, and on this particular morning had decided instead to accompany Mr. Grimes on his investigation of all things Stormquell.

Grimes had no idea who was shadowing him, despite Brown's efforts to communicate. A little mental push every once in a while was all he could manage, which occasionally enabled him to pass on information from his fellow ghosts.

For example, the hirers of the removal company when Draken had decided to leave town. Mary and Mrs. Orsen had spotted the company's name on the side of the van and Mr. Grimes, thinking this was entirely his own idea, had followed the subsequent paper trail and was now sitting in the reopened Clifton's Cafeteria in Downtown Los Angeles, waiting for someone.

Brown sat nearby, looking this way and that. Downtown always unnerved him. Its continual cycles of boom and bust had left behind a plethora of disturbing phenomena. Some of the venerable old buildings had changed hands and occupations more than once. Banks had become book stores, theaters had become indoor markets before falling into ruin. Hotels had become neglected and creepy before being rescued and turned into apartments, while their neighboring administration buildings remained boarded up, awaiting redevelopment. As for the ghosts that occupied them, Brown's fingers were firmly crossed, hoping they didn't congregate for lunch at Clifton's on Broadway.

Thankfully, they didn't have long to wait. A woman approached with a tray containing a soda and a plate of green jello. She was skinny, her shoulders slightly hunched, wearing a blue jersey dress and her hair tucked behind a matching blue hair band. Brown estimated her age at mid-forties, and she glanced uneasily over her shoulder before taking a seat.

"I shouldn't be here."

"It's good to see you, Grace. I know you're taking a risk, but thank you all the same." Grimes had risen briefly as she'd arrived and was now smiling wolfishly. Obviously, he was pulling out all the stops. Brown settled down to listen at the next table.

The woman took a sip of her soda. "How long have you had a ghostly companion?" She nodded toward Brown who raised an eyebrow. He hadn't sensed anything about her that would suggest she could see him, although he was beginning to realize it didn't always work out the way he expected.

Grimes appeared baffled for a moment. "An older man, wearing a brown coat?" And when Grace nodded, "That would be Mr. Brown, our former caretaker who died some months ago." He squinted vaguely in Brown's direction. "That you Gregory?"

Brown regarded the woman. "Can you hear me?" He was rewarded with a brief smile before her furtive glances returned.

"I'm assuming he's friend and not foe?" She pushed a large brown envelope across the table. "This is all I could get on Mr. Carl Drake."

"Thank you," Grimes said. "The more we can discover—"

"I think you'll find our company has known something of their client's nature for quite a while. Some of this information goes back years, in case you were wondering."

"How long?"

"The earlier deeds go back to the 1910s, which for this city is pretty far back."

"Good God, how long as he been here?"

The woman named Grace tucked delicately into her lime jello. "Longer than you thought, obviously."

At the next table Brown slowly nodded to himself. Somehow it fit, especially after listening to some of the conversations between his fellow ghosts on the subject.

There's always been a dragon.

Which begged the question, when did Draken and Reave become acquainted? Reave was in her thirties, maybe a pristine forty-year-old, but no more than that, or so it appeared. He needed to stop taking things at their face value.

"By the way," Grace added, "The two properties for sale in Laurel Canyon? They were withdrawn ten days after they were listed. Seems someone had a change of heart."

Grimes frowned. "What do you make of that?"

"Hard to say. Properties are withdrawn all the time. Maybe their initial market information didn't bear out."

The conversation shifted to small talk. Brown remained at the next table, chewing over what he'd just heard. Had Draken thrown up the sale as a smoke screen? Maybe the wily old rascal had moved right back in. What had Rogan said? That he was an artist, with a cat and two dogs? Did it mean the sigils would be replaced? And what about Reave? He still hadn't plucked up the nerve to talk to Caroline Aldred. He'd tell his fellow ghosts, he decided. Together, they could keep tabs on the place if nothing else.

The meeting over, he accompanied a distracted Mr. Grimes a few streets north to where they'd parked the Lincoln in Little Tokyo. They passed by a row of homeless tents and an old church that had been used in an eighties horror movie. The place looked spruced up, someone had hung banners outside, and yet it still seemed spooky and slightly off-kilter, and Brown was happy Mr. Grimes was setting a fast pace.

When they reached the car and Grimes had buckled up, "If you're still here, Gregory, when we get back I'll grab the kid and we'll go through these documents."

Brown nodded and settled in the passenger seat. At least, via Lennox, they'd be able to talk.

"And by the way," his companion added. "About Grace. It's not what you think, and I'm probably talking to myself, right now." He continued to mutter to himself on the remainder of the journey. Brown understood his frustration but there was nothing he could do until they'd gotten back, so he tuned out and let the other man ramble until they arrived at the Rothe house, where young Lennox was able to join them and help create a proper conversation.

"Regarding Grace, he says he doesn't believe you and thinks you're a wily old fox," was the boy's first contribution.

Grimes rolled his eyes and brought forth the

envelope he'd acquired earlier. He and Lennox had carried a couple of stools and a small, foldaway table outside the gate so as to display the envelope's contents and discuss what they contained.

"That's quite a list of properties," Brown mused. Stormquell, it seemed, had amassed a considerable portfolio.

Grimes stabbed a finger. "That's the derelict site where they dumped Rogan. A recent acquisition. I wonder what they're up to?"

"Which one is Draken?" Lennox asked. He was looking at a photograph of five men dressed in business suits.

Brown pointed. "Him, maybe? He's the only one with gray hair."

They were interrupted by Rogan arriving in the truck. Brown watched him climb out of the cab and remove a box containing a chainsaw from the truck bed.

"That looks ominous."

Rogan offered him a wink. "All the better to deal with Mrs. Aldred."

"What?"

"He's promised to clear out her yard," Lennox said, grinning at Brown's expression, one that took a while to dissipate while he considered the implications.

"Does this mean I'm off the hook?"

"Yep." Rogan placed the box alongside the gate and

approached the table. Grimes backed off, allowing the other man to look at the documents. They all watched eagerly as he picked up the photo. "Son of a bitch."

"What is it?" Lennox was tiptoeing to get a better look.

"He's holding a drink in his left hand."

Brown and Lennox got it immediately, whereas it took Grimes a moment or two.

"This photo may have been transposed," he said.

"I'm betting it hasn't." Rogan approached the truck. He leaned forward against the tailgate and closed his eyes.

"It wouldn't surprise me at all if his deformity is a ruse," Brown said. He remembered Rogan telling him about his encounter with Draken, and they'd considered the creature would be less of a threat if he couldn't fly. But if he'd been pretending...

"Let's examine the photo and make absolutely sure before we start contemplating the end of the world," Grimes scolded. He gathered up the papers, stuffed them in their envelope and went off in search of Dr. Halberd.

"This is bad, isn't it?" Lennox said.

Rogan didn't answer. His eyes were still closed and he was rubbing the bridge of his nose.

"There's nothing we can do about it now," Brown said. "We stick to our plan, and take things one step at a time." For the boy's sake his voice carried as much fortitude as he could muster, but he had to admit, if they had a fully functional dragon on their hands, then the stakes had certainly risen.

We'll handle it, he vowed silently, and offered the boy a reassuring smile.

3

ROGAN

With no other choice but to pull himself together, Rogan got on with the business of the afternoon which was a walk-through of Caroline's front yard in order to determine where to start. He was aware of her presence as he climbed through the undergrowth, and once or twice he caught a glimpse of her watching him from an upstairs window.

Gradually, as he'd already done with the Rothe house, he began to recognize a layout beneath the tangle. A brick path that led across the front of the house. Raised beds that had contained roses, their root stock having long since taken over. He let himself become absorbed by the task while the terrifying notion of a fully-functional Draken continued to haunt him.

Retired, my ass, offered the snake.

Although, it shouldn't have come as a surprise. His audience with Jake's brother, Jerrad, had strongly suggested that Draken couldn't be trusted.

After an hour of taking notes and stumbling through the tangle, he arrived at the front of the house and looked up toward the broken windows. "Mrs Aldred?" He nearly jumped out of this skin as she materialized alongside him, her bitter aura souring the air.

"You're about to tell me of all the noise you'll make."

"The chainsaw. I'll also need help removing the debris. I talked to Mr. Hernandez in town."

Her laughter was dismissive. "You really think they would dare set foot in here? And do you think I'd let them?"

He was prepared for this. "I figured on a compromise. If I can haul everything toward the gate —" He stopped, for she'd vanished, and when he turned around he saw her standing twenty feet away.

"This is the boundary. They must never come any closer than this."

Rogan expressed a sigh of relief. Most of the heavier stuff, the palms, some of the more ungainly shrubs, were growing determinedly outside the boundary she had specified. As for the assertion that any men hired wouldn't step beyond the gate, well, he'd just have to turn on the charm, maybe hand over more money, and hope it worked.

She remained outside as he continued, following him at a short distance while he decided on tools and debris removal in the most unobtrusive manner possible.

"How do you feel about sunlight?" he asked her at one point. "Once those trees are cut down it'll be a whole lot lighter."

"It will bring life into the house," she said. "Something I can no longer do."

"Oh, I don't think—"

"Don't insult me with cheap flattery."

Rogan winced. "Sorry."

"As you should be." She was about to continue berating him when a heavy esoteric blanket dropped over the entire neighborhood. "The Khir'gham," she said, and folded her arms across her chest.

"Yes, ma'am." He looked toward the Rothe house where Jake had now emerged from the tunnel that led into Palladium. No doubt he'd be heading directly to his room and wouldn't emerge until nightfall.

Then what? asked the snake who'd awakened from a temporary slumber.

Resigning himself to being pulled in two directions, Rogan consulted his notes. He'd get the palm trees felled first, that way there'd be some immediate progress, and he told his ghostly companion.

"Very well," was all she said and drifted back inside the house.

The sun was now falling rapidly so he called it quits, returned to his cottage, and washed up ready for dinner.

"How did you get on?" Mrs. Harris asked a short while later, bringing a large tureen of broth to the table.

Rogan broke off a piece of soda bread from a thick loaf in front of him. "Okay, I think. I'm still here, so that's a plus."

The housekeeper tut-tutted. "I've no sense of her at all, but if she's that dangerous, this gardening agreement might not be in your best interests, Mr. Moore."

"I'll be fine." He smiled and hoped he sounded more confident than he felt.

Across the table, Lennox was absorbing everything and thankfully not asking any questions. Talk ceased as they ate dinner and the subject of Jake's arrival was kept at bay. For half an hour at least, here were three ordinary people sitting at the table eating dinner.

However, back outside on his way to the cottage, his blissful sense of ordinariness was swept aside as he saw Jake's silhouette in one of the house's upper windows. What his arrival meant, he had no clue, but he hoped he wasn't about to be dragged immediately back into Palladium. They had some talking to do first, primarily about Draken.

He raised his hand and waved. Jackal, Khir'gham Guardian of the Void, waved back.

Leaving his door unlocked, for a couple of hours he lay awake, fully expecting an insistent knocking, or for Jake to simply burst in and drag him off on another hair-raising adventure. Instead, he woke the following morning undisturbed.

Bemused, he headed out for breakfast while the other man's presence felt so strong, it was as if he was sitting alongside him as he chowed down on scrambled eggs, toast, and pancakes. He said nothing to Lennox and Mrs. Harris, preferring to listen as they discussed the boy's lessons for the day, comprehension and geometry by the sound of it, banal subjects that wouldn't fill Lennox's head with ideas about sneaking off into Palladium or climbing the wall into next door.

Afterward, he finished off a few chores around the house before stepping outside, just in time to see Mr. Hernandez's men rumbling up the hill in a large truck, followed closely by a well-used cherry picker and tree shredder. A few minutes of negotiation followed, a bonus fee was agreed upon due to the otherworldly presence surrounding the Italianate, and he had to hand it to them. They had the trees out, chopped and shredded in under two hours, and not a squeak from the lady of the manor who had chosen to keep her distance.

When the men had gone he stood in the middle of the Italianate's front yard and marveled at the transformation. It was approaching late afternoon and the sun was already hiding behind the eucalyptus. Nonetheless, gentle light filtered through thin, shimmering leaves and bathed the yard in gentle light. The effect was magical, while the tree removal made the area in front of the house seem twice its previous size.

A grin on his face, he turned toward the house, hoping Caroline would come outside and take a look, only to discover she was already here. She was standing some ways to his left, her eyes closed and her arms raised toward the sun as if bathing in the light. Not knowing what else to do, he stood and stared.

"Leave me," she hissed. "Go, now."

"Yes, ma'am."

Quickly, he gathered his tools and left via the front gate, closing it carefully behind him. Her tone had forbidden any conversation, and he had no idea if the tree removal had been a success or not, until Brown appeared alongside him as he walked back toward the Rothe house gate.

"What did you just do?"

Rogan shrugged. "We felled a few trees."

Brown laughed. "Can't you feel it?" And when Rogan looked baffled, "It's like it's her birthday and you've just given her the perfect gift."

He looked back at the Italianate, entirely bemused.

"I'm betting she won't like it when you disappear into Palladium, though," Brown continued. "Still, this is a good sign."

"Any news on Draken?"

"Not yet, other than the houses are still empty." And after a moment of hesitation, "Just be careful, Rogan. Remember whom you're dealing with."

He was about to ask the former caretaker to elaborate when he heard Dr. Halberd calling. Immediately, Brown faded from view.

Halberd was at the top of the front steps, insistently beckoning. "Jake is in the library. He wants to see you."

"Not like him to rise this early."

"No. But I'm assuming it's important." Halberd seemed on edge.

Frowning, Rogan entered the house, and it wasn't until he was half way across the hall that he became reacquainted with Jake's oppressive aura and their psychic connection. Had he been *that* distracted by the events of the afternoon? His renewed insight also told him the guardian wasn't in the best of moods, which explained Dr. Halberd's behavior, just now. His temper on the rise, Rogan entered the library without knocking.

Just keep your mouth shut, scolded the snake. *Let's see what he has to say.*

Accepting the creature's advice, he closed the door behind him and waited.

Jake was standing alongside one of the bookcases, holding an open book which Rogan knew he wasn't reading, and after he placed it slowly and deliberately back on the shelf, "The entity in the next house. I see you're becoming acquainted."

"Mrs. Aldred, yes. I'm hoping she'll tell me what happened to Reave."

"You realize the effect she's having?"

"No." Rogan's frown returned. "Is it a problem?"

"I don't know, is it?"

"What's the matter, Jake? I didn't come running fast enough?" A shallow table alongside the hearth was tugging at his attention, and when he looked he saw Dr. Halberd's special box, the one they'd used to carry the worm into Palladium, sitting on top of it.

Quite involuntarily he took a step back. The box sat there like a threat, and immediately he knew something bad was coming.

Jake's smile was cold. "I want to show you something."

"You've said that before."

"Why are you afraid? This is nothing compared to the hounds, which you dealt with admirably."

And yet, I still feel them inside me. "What is it?"

"A construct. Like the worm."

"Except it isn't. Not quite."

The other man nodded. "I was worried you were so preoccupied you'd be unable to tell the difference."

"Okay, when?"

"Before dinner or after, your choice."

"Before, although if we're going outside, we might have an audience."

Jake smiled again. "It doesn't matter. Shall we?" He collected the box.

Glad you chose now, offered the snake. *Better to get it over with.*

Rogan wasn't so sure. He felt a strong need to get away as fast as he could, despite having run before, only to drop himself into a bigger tangle of horrors.

Outside, stepping beyond the sanctuary of the gate, he discovered no sign of Gregory Brown, or any of the other ghosts who had chosen to hang out there on occasion.

"No wraiths?" Jake asked while setting the box on a nearby wall.

"No. How come?" He saw the other man about to open the container. "Wait. Can we talk this over, first?"

Jake ignored him. "I'd rather you examined this

with no preconceptions." He flipped the lid and a matte black creature the size of a fat raccoon sprang forth and hit the ground on six short, stumpy legs.

"What the hell is that?"

"A construct. If it was a different color one might mistake it for a burrower. They hide beneath the sand in the shallows of our oceans."

Rogan took a step back as it advanced. "Where's its head?"

Jake said nothing. Instead, the creature opened a wide mouth at what Rogan thought was its rear end, extending a long, thick tongue that lashed out and encircled his right ankle.

Cursing, he crouched and grabbed the beast, spreading his fingers until they sank beneath its flesh. Immediately, it disintegrated and pieces of it floated before him like a collection of lazy moths. He looked down at his ankle. Thankfully, his foot was still attached, but there was residual pain and he winced.

Jake was sighing with impatience while his fingers were dancing, putting the creature back together. "Destroying it wasn't the object of this."

"Hey, it bit me, or stung me, or whatever those creatures do." He watched as the beast became whole once more. It let out an angry screech.

"Control it," Jake said. "It shouldn't be difficult." His face carried a smirk as if he was enjoying Rogan's discomfort.

The critter advanced once more and this time,

when it opened wide, he caught a glimpse of its smoky interior.

"I should have kept you with me," Jake continued. "You've forgotten everything I taught you."

Rogan was slowly backing away. "Take it easy, your lordship. I told you we should have talked about this first." Whatever a burrower was, he hoped never to meet a real one. In the meantime, he recalled something Reave had said before she'd betrayed him.

The Void loves you, Rogan.

But there was no love here. His ankle still throbbed, courtesy of the burrower's raspy tongue.

Remember, it's a construct, scolded the snake.

Except I've never constructed anything. I've only destroyed it. And there lay the conundrum.

The thing lashed out and once more grabbed his ankle in exactly the same spot as before, delivering a worse sting. Rogan glared at Jake who was watching the entire debacle. Mentally, the guardian was leaning on him like a brick wall, while the creature's grip had tightened so much his foot was becoming numb.

A construct. He remembered how pieces of the Void floated around him in its rawest form. Perhaps a slight disruption of its current integrity, followed by redirection. Simple enough in theory, but in practice, once again the thing fell to pieces. "Tell you what, while I'm figuring this out, why don't you tell me about Draken?"

"I hardly think this is the time—"

"I can't do this while you're crushing the inside of my head."

Jake frowned, but he backed off. "What do you want to know?" His fingers got busy, putting his horrific creation back together.

"I want to know the personal stuff, how long have you known him? Are you friends or enemies?"

"It matters?" A few flicks of the wrist and he was done.

"It matters."

"And yet the words friend and enemy are meaningless when discussing Draken."

"Hope you're not about to tell me they're exclusive to humanity. Because the more I see of you guys, the more human you become."

Jake laughed. "You're referring to my brother's concerns."

"Jerrad? Yes. We both think Draken is up to no good." He crouched low and watched the creature approach. "Don't forget he lied to you about Reave, and he also lied to me about his decrepitude. The question is, why? If he starts flying around, breathing fire—"

"And now you're being ridiculous." Jake offered him a triumphant smile.

"It's not funny—"

"Silence. Look at what you've done." He gestured to the creature.

Rogan saw it was crouched alongside him, panting softly like a pet dog. "I didn't—"

"Yes, you did."

Disruption. Redirection. His subconscious had taken care of it while he was lecturing Jake about his treacherous cousin. "I see you managed to get the smoke on the inside."

Jake grinned. "I did. I used your suggestion regarding the wraiths and did some experimenting."

"I hope no wraiths were hurt."

"Would it matter if they were?" And when Rogan looked horrified, "Wraiths are remnants. Their lives are over."

"But how—?"

"The Void is physical, whereas wraiths draw their power from spiritual energy. It does require a certain mindset. A combination of the two—"

"Like mind and body, you mean?" He crouched and extended his arm, allowing the creature to crawl forth until it was perched on his shoulder. It felt light and cold sitting there, reminding him of a figment. When he stood, he felt the creature's feet digging in while retaining its balance. "You were about to tell me about Draken."

The other man frowned. "What you asked will be difficult to explain. It's not a question of friendship and I can't really refer to him as a cousin." He raised a hand and the creature perched on Rogan's shoulder retracted its claws and began to float through the air toward him. A further gesture and it curled into a ball and returned to the box.

"Draken was the very first," he continued. "Palladium's sole protector. There was little need for me and my cousins until something happened and the Void grew stronger."

"So, what you're saying is, he was part of a different world?"

Jake flicked the catches on the box, securing the lid. "Yes, and there was no need for guardians. It was only later when the Sisters decided—"

"Wait, are you telling me he could control the Void, like you?" And after Jake nodded, "Well that certainly explains where Reave got her expertise."

"Do you really think he taught her? I don't see an advantage—"

"I do. She does his dirty work while he can get on with whatever he's doing here with a clear conscience."

"Remember, we don't think like you."

"Sure you don't." Rogan grinned, feeling positively lightheaded now the construct was back in its box. "What did you guys talk about?"

Jake let out a sigh. He leaned on the wall and folded his arms across his chest. "He talked, I listened, mostly."

"About what?"

Freedom, futility, changing direction." He

shrugged when Rogan looked confused. "I told you it wouldn't be easy to explain. Not only that, his experiences are different to those of mine. Perhaps Jerrad would make more sense of it. Then again, perhaps not."

"Can I offer you my thoughts?"

"After the one conversation you had."

"Look, I don't know what you guys talked about. It sounds like some kind of philosophical bullshit, but let me tell you, he lied to me. And yet, right at the very last minute he offered me a glimpse of his power. He really didn't need to do that. But it told me he was throwing down a challenge, something you love to do, by the way."

Jake picked up the box. "I challenge you, Rogan, because your mind isn't always where it should be."

"Okay, then let's extend that thought to you and Draken. Maybe he's throwing down the same gauntlet."

"He talked of... possibilities."

"And now we're getting somewhere. Is he attempting to recruit you?"

"For what?"

"You tell me, and don't look so surprised."

"Rogan, my duty, and my purpose, are forever attached to what you call Palladium."

"Telenth is having doubts about you though, isn't he? All this time spent in the forbidden world."

"Enough. This is something I need to discuss with Jerrad and is not for your ears."

"Except, don't forget I'm the Nembraean emissary, now."

Jake pointed. "The gate?"

Rogan depressed the latch and followed the guardian back toward the house. Body language informed him of the man's irritation, but despite being touted as the most powerful, Jake seemed horrifically naïve.

Unlike you? offered a sarcastic snake.

"We leave tomorrow night," Jake said as he climbed the concrete steps. "So I suggest, *Emissary*, you get your affairs in order as soon as possible."

Rogan remained at the base of the steps and watched him disappear into the house, breathing a sigh of relief once he'd gone. He'd known this was coming, and wondered how the ghost next door would take the news.

It had been a pity Brown hadn't shown his face. Hopefully, he'd pop out of nowhere tomorrow and they could discuss the best course of action regarding their troublesome neighbor.

It was twilight now and he could only see the dull silhouette of the eucalyptus swaying in the breeze. On cue, his stomach rumbled for sustenance and he headed to the kitchen for dinner.

4

BROWN

In the growing darkness Brown remained where he was, standing behind the thick trunk of a tree some ways down the street, from where he'd watched Rogan and the guardian playing with their new toy.

To say he'd been repulsed by the crawling little horror was an understatement. The worm had been bad enough, and even though he'd successfully conquered his fear of it, this new creation took his distaste to a whole new level.

Staring at it long enough had brought exhaustion, reminding him of what Foster and the others had told him about their sapped energy. And whereas the worm hadn't affected him all that much, this latest creature had made it blatantly obvious it would suck the life out of him if he ventured too close.

He wondered if Rogan had sensed the differences. Brown had watched him grow from abhorrence to mastery of the creature in such a short space of time. He'd witnessed the man's aura flicker and grow brighter. What it meant, Brown had no idea, but it couldn't be good.

His thoughts weighed heavy, threatening to drag him into despair until they were distracted by a voice singing a light melody. Edging from the trees he drifted toward the Italianate, and after a moment's hesitation he climbed the fence.

The yard beyond looked vastly different after the gardeners had done their work. A thick cluster of trees and vegetation had been entirely removed, opening up a considerable amount of space, and it was within that space he saw Caroline Aldred.

She was as robust as he had ever seen her. The dreadful aura that usually clung to her seemed diminished, and there she was, singing to herself in this new open space, dancing until her skirts swirled around her feet.

Fully captivated, Brown stared. He couldn't help himself. In the meantime he noticed she was surrounded by a number of twinkling lights, like tiny stars. It was a magical moment he had no wish to sour, and slowly, carefully, he climbed down from his perch.

"Huh," was all he managed before heading toward

the Rothe house gate in order to settle in for his nightly vigil. And for a while he sat and pondered these latest events, until an hour or two later he was joined by Mary and Liebermann from the Franklin crowd.

"There was a man at one of the dragon's houses, today," Liebermann said. "He met someone outside, a house sitter."

"Were you able to go inside?"

Both ghosts nodded. "From what we could overhear, the house sitter is to stay for a month and oversee deliveries."

"What kind of deliveries?"

"We don't know, but we can always watch and see what happens."

Brown nodded, his mood sinking. As far as he was concerned they were back facing a heap of jigsaw pieces that refused to slot together, and the more he thought about it the more disconsolate he grew.

Later, when the others had gone and the mistress next door had stopped singing he decided to re-visit Reave's empty house in Laurel Canyon. He discovered a light on in one of the upper windows, and on closer inspection saw a number of crates had been delivered and were stacked outside the patio doors that led to the kitchen.

There were no vehicles in the garage and the house's sole occupant, thankfully not the killer twins, was a voluptuous and very attractive young woman with teal hair.

He hung out for a while, trying to remain inconspicuous, but other than the girl making a cup of hot chocolate and retiring to bed with a TV show and her laptop there was nothing else going on and in the end he decided to call it a night.

On his way out he noticed a small, blocky logo stamped on one of the crates. Stormquell Industries was spelled out in thick letters, hovering above a cloud shot through with a lightning bolt. The other crates carried the same logo which suggested something was definitely afoot. It was another puzzle piece, one he stacked with the rest.

5

ROGAN

On arrival at the dock in Jake's home sector of Ellised, they were met by Jake's companions, Loya and Sabal, who were accompanied by two others, a man and a woman wearing decidedly brighter garb.

"These are your new aides," Jake told him after the requisite bowing was done with, and while Rogan stood dumbfounded he added, "You'll go with them to the palace while I return home with this." He handed Halberd's ornamental box to Sabal. "Don't be concerned. We'll meet up later." And while Rogan was still summoning up a suitable complaint, Jake climbed aboard a carriage with his companions and was soon swallowed up by the bustling city.

"Emissary, we have our own carriage waiting," the woman said. Her name was Ellin, slightly taller than the man who offered his name as Dann.

Bewildered and trying desperately not to show it, he allowed them to lead him to the carriage and Jerrad's ostentatious domain. He remembered hardly anything from his past visit, but as he walked through countless hallways and up numerous flights of stairs, the journey sought to remind him of the terrible events in another palace, where two other aides and their grandparents had been brutally murdered. By the time they reached his chambers he felt decidedly uneasy.

Inside, they were met by another woman. This one was a little older, her hair woven with multi-colored ribbons, wearing a dark blue gown at odds with the colorful dresses he'd seen on everyone else.

"Emissary, I am Seril," she said, her voice deep and smooth as velvet.

Rogan nodded. "Thank you," he told them, "and please, call me Rogan, all of you."

Having got that out of the way, they gave him a tour of his apartments. There were multiple rooms, opulent rugs, vases full of richly colored flowers. Beyond a huge swathe of gauze curtains was a balcony that offered a spectacular view of the city. However, amidst his perusal of the city's sparkling rooftops he sensed something was wrong.

"I've seen you before," he told Seril. "You beckoned

me into Jerrad's quarters that day when—" he stumbled over the next few words, struggling for context in this foreign language. "I'm sorry this is a demotion for you. I'll try not to make things difficult."

She seemed surprised. "They told me you were perceptive. Should this get back to his Excellency—"

"It won't, I assure you."

The woman smiled faintly. "Then we need to get you washed and changed into proper attire. You have a meeting with the Ellised emissary directly after lunch."

There was a terrible moment when he thought he'd have to renege on his promise, that the proper attire would involve gaudy colors and lots of fabric. Thankfully, they appeared to have the measure of him, and after a delicious lunch they had him dressed in a white shirt, black pants and boots, and he was allowed to keep the black jacket he'd acquired on his last visit.

Awash with relief, he even allowed them to mess endlessly with his hair until it was tamed to their satisfaction. Then it was off to see Ellised's emissary, Frey, whom he vaguely remembered from their meeting at Jake's house.

Not knowing what to expect, or what was expected of him, his dismay grew once they'd been left alone and a cup of plum wine had been placed in his hand.

"So, how do you intend to save our worlds from the chaos inspired by Excellency Draken?" Frey was an older woman with a demeanor that suggested she wasn't to be messed with. Dressed in rich crimson, her robe decorated with flowers and birds, she was a distinguished figure, her current manner amplifying Rogan's position as gauche newcomer.

"Ma'am, right now I have no idea."

"Well, at least you're being honest, although it begs the question, why did Excellency Jerrad appoint you? Were there no other suitable persons available?"

"I'm here to learn everything I can," he offered.

"I'm told you had an audience with Draken. Something only our ancestors have enjoyed. What was he like?"

Rogan took a drink from his wine cup and thought carefully about what he should say. "I've never met anyone like him. He offered me a façade. Perhaps he was worried my head would explode."

She smiled. "Stormkeepers take some getting used to."

"And yet he's more than that, isn't he?"

"So legend has it."

"I've also heard the Sisters could help matters if they chose."

"The Sisters? What do you know of the Sisters?"

He regarded Frey uncomfortably. Again, what should he say? Oh, I once lay in the lap of a Sister while she brought me back to life? The emissary already thought he was full of it after he'd allegedly done something she had only dreamed about. An audience with the almighty Draken. He got the impression Frey considered the dragon a legendary figure who didn't really exist.

"Very little," he said eventually. "Tell me, Emissary, what is it you want from me?"

"I'm trying to get the measure of you. When Silas and I watched you bursting into Jerrad's room we assumed you were about to meet your demise. And yet, here you are, the Nembraean emissary."

"Still alive, still kicking." He smiled, hoping she'd lighten up. Instead, she shook her head and glared. "Would it help if I told you I share your concerns about our worlds, and I'll do what I can to ensure their safety?"

"It would help a great deal." She drained her glass. "Walk with me. I'll show you a little of the palace and the city."

"Is Excellency Jerrad here at present?" he asked as they left her quarters and headed downstairs.

"I suspect he'll be on the platform by now. We have a storm coming. You didn't choose the best time to pay us a visit."

"The platform?"

"You must have seen it when you arrived at the harbor."

"The tall column rising from the hills? I couldn't see the summit because of the clouds."

"It's rarely in view, but it gives his excellency the perfect viewpoint over the storm."

"I noticed the harbor was busy. Were all the boats coming in for shelter?"

"Undoubtedly, otherwise their cries for help would be aimed at the Sisters, and the Sisters rarely listen."

"I've seen him in flight. It was spectacular."

"Surely, you have similar?"

He thought about explaining an Airbus A380 but gave up. "Not like that."

As they walked he saw others stepping out of their way and inclining their heads. Uncomfortable, he distracted himself with the architecture. He'd been too anxious the last time and hadn't really noticed, whereas on this occasion he absorbed the differences in décor. There were none of the resplendent scenes depicted in Gherem's palace. Looking up, it was as if he was staring directly at a blue sky decorated with the occasional fluffy white cloud. The effect was to give light to the ceiling far above and it made him feel slightly dizzy.

"These are the skies we aspire to," Frey told him, "and the ones we pray for."

"Whom do you pray to?"

"Excellency Jerrad, of course."

They were approaching a polished marble hallway that bore columns at its far end. Beyond them he could see daylight and two of the city's shining turrets. On arrival at the balcony, the view was spectacular. The coast stretched ahead to his left, while the city's rooftops finally became scarce in the far distance. Closer, the harbor still looked busy. Two large ships were hastily being towed to their berths. Meanwhile, directly ahead, a wall of gray cloud was falling toward a range of tall mountains.

Squinting, he could just make out the base of the platform. Was the almighty Jerrad up there, now? He remembered the angry abrasions on the man's flesh, damage done from a previous storm.

"Jerrad told me this would be so much easier if Emeril were to share the task."

"Yes, but until our issues have been resolved..."

Rogan looked down toward the harbor, remembering the name of Emeril's domicile. "How would I get to Baccaned?"

Frey stared at him for a moment. "What? You think you can just walk in?"

He smiled. "Why not?"

"You might think you've faced the worst with Jerrad, and even Draken, but Emeril is unpredictable. He—" She paused as a small parade approached the palace directly below.

Rogan frowned as he shared her view. They were carrying a stretcher and the body lying upon it was completely covered.

"Ah," Frey whispered, "they already found Jerrad's

chosen."

"I'm sorry, what happened?"

"You truly don't know?"

Don't go asking her to explain, said the snake, abruptly coming awake. *You won't like it.*

Helplessly, he shrugged, while the worst possible scenario began to flower in his subconscious.

"But, I heard you gave yourself to Jackal," she continued, "during the attack beneath Tyfohwed."

"I didn't give. He took. There's a difference." He stared at the bier and its forlorn escort. "Is that what happened here? Are they dead?"

"Of course they're dead." Her voice had hardened, and she was looking at him as if he was a stupid child.

Rogan stepped back from the balcony and took a few deep breaths.

Get a grip, scolded the snake. *This should hardly come as a surprise.*

"How often does this happen?" he asked.

"I heard it used to be once every fifty storms," she said. "But now it's every ten. His excellency's mastery over them takes its toll."

He nodded grimly. "I've seen some of the damage done." Stepping back alongside his fellow emissary, he looked down, but there was no sign of the sorry little parade now. Just a city sparkling defiantly in the dimming light, attempting to go about its business in the face of catastrophe, while its citizens prayed quietly to the mighty creature atop the platform, poised to calm the raging storm at such terrible cost.

"If we can get Emeril back in the skies, will that number head back toward fifty? Could we save a few lives?"

"I'd like to think so, taking account of Emeril's subsequent consumption."

"Okay, I'll ask again. How do I get to Baccaned?"

"The dock, and they'll take you, no question. Protocol, however, insists that you at least let Emissary Silas know you're coming."

This is madness, said the snake. *And what about Jake? He might not let you go.*

Rogan wanted nothing more than to run down the palace's marble stairs, dash toward the harbor, and board a ship at all speed. Except he couldn't because the snake was right, and in all probability the harbor was closed because of the incoming storm. "I'll do that," he said, trying to remember who Silas was.

"Shall we continue?" Frey asked.

"Please, and forgive my ignorance. I'm already learning a great deal in your company."

They retreated and she led him to another hall with another balcony. This one gave them a better view of the city as a whole, and while Frey pointed out its various districts he remained silent while his mind stewed over the dead body on the stretcher and Draken. He remembered his discussion with Brown, about the possibility of young virgins being on the menu. It had been a flip comment and yet, the implications were there. Like the snake said, this shouldn't have come as a surprise. How many people had been sucked dry to heal that originally withered arm, for example?

A lightning flash brought him swiftly out of his melancholy. The sky had darkened considerably and heavy drops of rain were now falling.

"Do you wish to head back inside, or stay for a while?" Frey asked. "We're partially sheltered here."

"Stay, please?"

Others were gathering at the balustrade, their faces turned to the sky in order to watch the show.

"Blood and memories," Rogan whispered as another flash illuminated a mighty pair of wings, dancing within the churning clouds.

Emissary Frey raised an eyebrow but said nothing, and together they watched until the rain made the air inside the hall so thick with moisture they had no choice but to retreat in order to avoid being soaked.

Moments later he felt Jake on the approach. Emissary Frey sensed it too, and together they waited.

The guardian was alone. He was wearing a long overcoat that billowed behind him. He looked as if he'd just walked out of the storm.

"Excellency Jackal." Frey inclined her head.

"Emissary, I hope he hasn't been giving you any trouble?"

Rogan stayed silent and attempted to gauge the other man's mood. It was tense, troubled, but not aimed at him so he kept his mouth shut. He wanted Jake in a good mood so he'd agree to go to Baccaned.

However, after a few pleasantries, and having extracted Rogan from his fellow emissary's clutches, Jake gave him the bad news. "We have a potential problem which we need to investigate."

"Is it in Baccaned?"

"No."

"Don't you consider Emeril not doing his fair share a big enough problem?"

"Yes, but as problems go, I suspect this will be greater. As for Emeril, don't get too ahead of yourself."

Frowning, Rogan looked back toward the end of the hall where rain was still falling. "We'll have to wait for the storm—"

"No, we go now. I assume you're acquainted with the need for urgency?"

"What do I need?"

"Warmer clothing. See to it. There'll be a carriage waiting at the front entrance."

Rogan watched the other man walk away using a brisk pace. Meanwhile, a short distance away, Frey was still hovering and must have overheard the conversation, but she had nothing to add and merely shrugged.

Miraculously, he found his way back to his own

apartments, where Dann produced a long, hooded coat that bore subtle embroidery at its lower edges.

"I'm not sure when I'll be back," he said after thanking his aides.

Seril's smile was polite. "We'll be ready, Emissary."

Rogan got the impression they were glad he was out of their hair. He walked fast, all the while wondering what Jake was about to throw at him. The guardian's behavior hadn't been easy to read, once again suggesting that their time apart had perhaps severed a few ties. As for this latest issue, hopefully it wouldn't keep him away too long from Caroline Aldred's yard renovations, although by way of recompense he'd left her a gift before heading down the Rothe house ladder. He'd discovered another photograph in Halberd's album, this time containing a shot of Mr. And Mrs. Aldred, standing outside the front door of their new home. Consequently, he'd dashed into town, had the picture enlarged, and it was now framed and propped against the Italianate's porch. Fingers crossed it had the desired effect.

Things are piling up, offered the snake.

Indeed they were.

6

BROWN

Another day and another quick trip in daylight to Reave's erstwhile empty house in Laurel Canyon, and having seen nothing more exciting than more deliveries of crates, Brown returned to the Rothe house at 11 a.m. with Foster in tow.

"Maybe they're growing weed," Foster said. "It won't be the only place in the canyon being converted for that purpose."

Brown was unconvinced. It didn't seem Draken's style, regardless of the fact that he didn't know what a dragon's style was. Over by the Italianate, one of their fellow ghosts, Mrs. Orsen, was beckoning.

"Come look at this," she hissed, "quickly, before

she notices we're here."

Glancing at Foster, who shrugged, Brown crept forward and rose above the fence until he could see into the Italianate's yard. Caroline Aldred had her back turned but he noticed the differences immediately. Gone was the drab, gray dress. In its place was a dark blue, full-length gown, while her hair was perfectly rolled and pinned on top of her head. She seemed more three-dimensional, too, more so than the night before, while her aura had become a rainbow of colors.

Having witnessed Rogan deliver a framed photograph before he left for Palladium, Brown explained.

"Enabling her to remember her better self," Foster mused.

"I didn't know you could do that," Mrs. Orsen said, looking down at herself. "Change, I mean. I might give it a try."

Brown wasn't sure if the changes were for better or worse. The shift in the witch's aura suggested a renewed strength and a certain amount of unpredictability.

"Anyway, I'm glad you're here," Orsen continued. "I think I've found him." She offered them both a triumphant smile.

"Draken?" Brown regarded her with astonishment.

"Yes. Follow me." Immediately, she disappeared.

Foster took a step back. "I'm sorry," he mumbled,

"I don't think I'm ready."

"It's all right. Chasing after dragons isn't for everyone."

His few seconds of hesitation were enough to make the following of Mrs. Orsen's trail difficult. She and the others had a tendency to forget he was still relatively new to this, and whatever he made up for in strength, it was easily offset by his cluelessness.

Abruptly, he found her voice and pushed toward it, arriving on a coastal path alongside a beautiful stretch of shoreline.

"Isn't it gorgeous? Our parents used to bring us up here when we were children and this place wasn't even built back then."

Having no idea where they were, Brown followed her pointing finger toward short concrete steps that rose between terraces and led to an expansive white-walled building with a shallow, terracotta roof. The sound of waves breaking on the shore collided with voices up ahead, further disorienting him.

"It's a hotel," Orsen said gleefully. "A very expensive one."

"But where the hell are we?"

"Just north of Santa Barbara. Come," she beckoned.

Grumbling, he followed. Mrs. Orsen had been a fourth grade teacher in the fifties and her nasty demise due to breast cancer hadn't dampened her ebullient demeanor. Neither had it stopped her from addressing her fellow ghosts as if they were her students. Her manner was annoying as hell, but if she was right...

At the top of the steps they arrived at a gathering. Tables were set out across a stretch of lawn, their surfaces cluttered with rumpled napkins and half-empty glasses. People were already on their feet, gathered in clusters. Others were walking up the steps to the main building, while the shallow stage erected at the far edge of the lawn was empty.

"Whatever this was," Brown said, "I think we missed it." No auras that he could detect in the gathering, either. No one special at all.

Mrs. Orsen was dashing ahead of him, following those who were climbing the steps. They passed by a sign perched on an easel that said Private Party, and he was a few paces from the hotel patio doors when he became aware.

The effect was a slight roll in his imaginary innards, as if he'd eaten something that hadn't agreed with him, reminding him of the sensation he'd felt while waiting for Rogan outside Draken's house all those weeks ago.

His companion had paused and was looking at him expectantly. After nodding his assent they passed through the doors into a wide hallway where more people were gathered.

Carl Drake was standing at the far end, talking to three women who were gazing at him in total adoration. And who wouldn't? The man, or at least he looked like a man at present, was over six feet tall, had a mane of white hair, a classically handsome face, and was a snappy dresser. Polished shoes, black pants, a beautifully tailored Prince-of-Wales check jacket. Even at this distance he oozed charisma and his three companions were lapping it up.

Mrs. Orsen was looking uncharacteristically wary. "He can't do us any harm, can he?"

"Not that I'm aware of," Brown said, "but I don't want to risk anything that'll send him after Rogan by way of retaliation."

"We'll be careful." Orsen edged forward. "Looking at how the women are dressed I'd say this was a very exclusive get-together."

Brown had no clue about women's clothing, but going off the surroundings he was willing to bet the parking spaces outside were full of expensive cars.

They passed by a placard that bore the Stormquell logo. Its smaller print contained the words 'exclusive invitation' and 'opportunities'. "Sounds like a fundraiser," he whispered as they crept closer.

"Well, I can certainly imagine him getting those ladies to part with their money. He looks straight out of a romance novel."

If the situation hadn't been so fraught with tension he'd have burst out laughing. Instead, he wished he was elsewhere, preferably back at the Rothe house. He couldn't remember who'd suggested this mad caper but it was a bad one.

"He's seen us," Orsen said a moment later.

"Are you sure?"

Of course I'm sure."

Brown's hopes of getting away unseen fell rapidly. Same with his earlier bravado on discovering Draken's whereabouts. The creature might have left his mansion in a hurry over a month ago but he wasn't exactly in hiding.

Two men walked by, one of whom Brown recognized as the extremely public face of a major dot-com company. His companion was an actor, also famous but perhaps not as rich, and after a short, genial conversation they left with their wives, no doubt rescuing them from Carl Drake's seductive clutches.

What followed was a terrifying moment when Drake faced them and beckoned before disappearing around a corner.

"Oh, this can't be good."

"Come on." Mrs. Orsen sounded as if she was scolding a small boy. "What do we have to lose?" She set off down the hallway at a ghostly but nonetheless brisk pace.

With no choice but to follow lest he make a fool of himself, he set off in her wake, silently cursing himself for being so afraid. As they rounded the corner they saw their quarry entering a room up ahead which turned out to be a small conference room with windows facing the ocean.

Drake had already taken a seat at the table and was pouring himself a glass of water from a carafe. "Come in, I don't bite. Not wraiths, anyway." His tone was genial but Brown wasn't buying it.

He watched Orsen take a seat opposite with no preamble, while he inclined his head and offered him the courtesy of "Excellency," before doing likewise.

For a moment they sat there while the dragon stared at them. Finally, Mrs. Orsen had had enough. "It's an honor to meet you, Mr. Drake—"

He silenced her by raising a finger. "Enough. Are you here at the behest of Jackal, or that powerful seer he holds on a leash?"

Brown and Orsen glanced at one another for a moment before Brown said, "We're here on behalf of the Rothe house—"

"Never heard of it, and I can smell the seer all over you. However, seeing as you're here you can tell me what happened to Reave, where she is, and what you intend to do about returning her to me." The implication in his voice rang loudly in Brown's ears.

If she's dead, God help you.

"We're attempting to discover her whereabouts, Sire." Inside, he was castigating himself for being a spineless weasel. Yes, Sire, no Sire, when he had important questions of his own like, What are you up to, Draken?

"I see. And as for whereabouts, I assume you'll be informing the seer as to mine? I've nothing to hide."

He spread his hands magnanimously.

"Why did you run?" It came out before Brown could stop himself. Mrs. Orsen glared at him. They were about to get thrown out for sure.

For a long moment Draken's fingers drummed the table. The smile had gone from that handsome face but there was no sign of the fury Brown was expecting.

"Ever had two Khir'gham guardians on your tail?" And after his ghostly visitors had stared in horror, "No, of course you haven't. They're immensely hard to kill and I had no idea how Jerrad would react." He leaned back in his chair and clasped his elegant fingers together. "Ask your seer what happened when *he* tried. Some confrontations are best avoided."

Mrs. Orsen managed to look mystified while still bristling at Brown. "Well," she said, "I'm sorry we took up so much of your time, and we wish you the very best in your endeavors." She stood and backed off.

Brown still had a long list of questions but she was right. If they were reading this correctly, this was about as far as they'd get. Again, he inclined his head as he stood. "Excellency."

"I'm relying on your discretion," Drake said as they were about to pass beyond the door. "It would be a shame to bring this fight to your doorstep."

As soon as they were outside the room, Orsen confronted him. "*Why did you run?* Why on earth did you say that? Good God, it's a wonder he didn't bite off our heads."

"Except we're wraiths. He can't do that."

"I wouldn't be so sure if I were you. Didn't you see what surrounded him? A creature with an aura like that—" She broke off for a moment and looked bewildered. "What do we do, now?"

"We tell Rogan. He'll know what to do."

"In the meantime, we've no idea where Draken lives."

"There's no need," he said, attempting to regain some authority. "If we keep an eye on Stormquell, we're keeping an eye on him. He obviously has an active role in the organization and I reckon we should see what they're up to, don't you?"

Orsen frowned at him for a moment before nodding reluctantly. "The big picture?"

"Precisely."

7

ROGAN

On their way to the dock, Rogan had the opportunity to witness how the city of Ellised coped with a sustained downpour. Deep, narrow channels were cut into either side of the street, catching water from the rooftops and gutters, carrying it away, he presumed, to the sea.

The air was thick with moisture beneath the canopied carriage and while he regretted not bringing his pistol, he was glad he'd packed an umbrella.

"What is that?" Jake had asked before Rogan had demonstrated by flicking the catch near the handle. "Oh, a portable canopy." They'd both huddled beneath it while dashing outside to their waiting ride.

When they alighted at the dock, Rogan didn't like the look of the water. It was already choppy inside the harbor wall. How would the ship fare once it had left its protective shelter?

He soon found out. Jake sensibly retired to his usual spot, the captain's cabin, in a ship vastly different to the others. This one was wider and bore a single mast. It also lacked a significant hold. Another look at the water and Rogan wondered how long he'd last before he was hurling his lunch over the side.

However, instead of plowing into more turbulent waters, as soon as they'd cleared the harbor the sail was re-furled, the ship tipped forward, and promptly plunged into a terrifying, dark channel. Clutching frantically at the rail, Rogan nearly fell overboard.

Seconds later they stopped falling and arrived in calmer waters, but it was so dark he couldn't see the horizon, while the sky above glittered dully like graphite.

"We'd be grateful for your observance, Emissary," the captain said.

"What are we looking for?" He was trying to appear nonchalant, as if hurtling down a dark chute was entirely commonplace.

"Disturbances in the water. Pray we don't get a visit from one of the Sisters." The man seemed to think his last sentence was funny and was laughing softly as he walked away.

Unsettled, Rogan gripped the rail and did as he

was asked, except anything beyond twenty feet was swallowed up in a black haze. The scene reminded him of the tunnel between the Quadrants and Tyfohwed.

At least we're not up top, bobbing around like a cork, offered the snake.

Loosening his fingers, he took a deep breath and tried to relax. He was a seer, and right now he wasn't seeing anything and therefore reasoned they were in the clear.

A short while later he was offered a hot, fruity drink and a combination of vegetables wrapped up like a burrito. Three hefty bites and the wrap was gone. The spices it contained warmed his innards.

Directly overhead, a woman was in the lookout singing a song, and he was part way through convincing himself the journey would prove uneventful when he heard a deep whooping sound that reverberated through the deck.

"Whales?" he asked a passing crew member.

"It's the Sisters, Emissary. No need to worry, they're quite distant."

Rogan wasn't so sure. He could see nothing out there and yet the sound had felt quite close. Still, what was there to worry about? One of them had brought him back to life once, and surely they wouldn't have gone to the trouble, only to kill him later?

The whale sound continued intermittently,

breaking an otherwise eerie silence. The singing stopped, the crew moved quietly about the ship and spoke in low tones.

Some time later, one of the male crew members arrived with a basket brimming with brightly-colored flower heads, reminding him of Mrs. Harris's dahlias that lined the edge of her vegetable patch. Rogan watched, fascinated, as the man threw the flowers overboard, one by one until they left a gaudy trail that receded into the darkness.

"For the Sisters?"

The man nodded, and as soon as he was done left him alone at the rail. Rogan kept his eyes on the flowers until they disappeared into the gloom.

A short while later his view became so monotonous he considered a change of viewpoint lest he fall asleep and topple into the water. But he remained where he was, listening to the whooping sounds emanating from the dark until he fancifully imagined some vast creature swimming directly beneath the vessel. Perhaps, if he stared hard enough, he would see a great eye regarding him before rolling and sinking into the depths. It was just his imagination, having a little fun after watching video clips of whale watchers and their close encounters.

A cold breeze at the back of his neck brought him out of his trance, and when he turned he saw the captain, Jake, and other crew members gathered nearby.

"What did I miss?"

"I told them not to disturb you," Jake said.

"Why? What's going on?"

The captain was on the verge of saying something until Jake silenced him with a look.

"It was nothing," the guardian continued.

Rogan wasn't buying it. He noticed the deck was wet below his feet, his clothing was soaked, too, which explained why he'd grown cold all of a sudden. And yet, his remaining senses felt distant. Was he asleep? Was he dreaming? The railing beneath his hand felt about to crumble beneath his fingers, and when he looked down he could no longer see it.

When he came to he was sitting alongside the mast, bundled in blankets. The environment had changed. The ship was gently pitching and the sky had shifted to a more agreeable tawny gray.

A dream then, right, snake?

Alas, his inner menace wasn't for talking.

Awkwardly, he stood and stretched. One of the crew offered him a bowl of hot soup which he gladly accepted, and on stepping to the railing he attempted to reorient himself. He felt perfectly dry, the wooden rail felt solid beneath his fingers and yet, his recent experiences still lingered.

There was no sign of Jake, the crew were keeping to themselves, and with nothing better to do he kept his eyes on the forward horizon which gradually shifted from a gray, incoherent mist to the vague, ghostly shells of distant buildings.

The structures loomed tall, growing sharper as the ship advanced, solidifying as they arrived at the dock. People dressed in long, thick coats moved silently along the quay, deftly catching the mooring ropes and tying them to the dock. Only then did Jake appear on deck, his face bearing a faraway look that bordered on reluctance.

Collecting his umbrella, Rogan approached. "What is this place?"

"Athed. The domain of Draken."

"But I thought—"

"Enough, Rogan. Wait until you've seen what we've come to see."

The crew seemed overly-courteous as they disembarked. Something was up, but Rogan was still feeling light-headed, inspiring him to remain silent and not kick up a fuss until he knew what they were dealing with.

On the quayside, as they headed for the city streets, he re-examined the buildings that had appeared so magically on approach. Close up, they appeared derelict and neglected, a far cry from the polished towers and painted walls of Nefhered and Ellised.

They passed by a blocky dwelling whose roof had collapsed. Lights shone dim in some of the windows, reminding him of the Quadrants, but even that sector of Palladium was in better shape than this. At the end of the quay a carriage was waiting, pulled by two giant hounds that looked poorly fed and ill-tempered. The driver appeared like his animals, with slumped shoulders and a sullen face.

Moisture hung heavy in the air as they set off through the streets. Rogan saw an occasional pedestrian here and there, who immediately ducked out of sight when they saw the carriage. It was a far cry from the citizens he'd seen elsewhere with their flowing robes of pink and orange. Jake was utterly silent alongside him, the faraway expression still on his face as if he'd folded into the landscape and partially disappeared.

Brief signs of life continued to appear. Narrow columns of smoke rising desultorily from chimneys. Smudges of light shining through dirty windows. But no real answers were forthcoming about the mood of the city until they reached the outskirts and the road began to follow the circumference of an enormous pit.

After one too many lurches over uneven ground, taking them horribly close to the edge, Rogan finally broke the silence. "I think I get it, now."

Jake closed his eyes, as if entirely disinterested in what he had to say, but Rogan was undeterred.

"All those fancy palaces and glittering towers, the materials had to come from somewhere, huh?" He looked out of the carriage into a chasm that had to be a mile wide. Part way down he saw movement, carts being pulled by people and animals. It made him remember the looks on the faces of those in the slave pens in the Quadrants, and yeah, he'd be miserable too, if this was his destination.

"Under normal circumstances I wouldn't have brought you here," Jake said, finally. "But we need to focus on what lies ahead."

"Oh, I can hardly wait to see what's worse than this."

"Don't tell me you don't have places like this at home."

"We—" He stopped talking.

Of course we do, said the snake, stating the obvious.

Rogan sank into his seat and folded his arms across his chest, entirely unhappy. He had no rebuttal. The snake was right. In fact some places were probably worse.

As their carriage continued around the lip of the pit, Rogan tried to catch a glimpse of what lay inside the carts but it was too dark down there, and shortly after they left the scene it started to rain. It wasn't the heavy downpour he'd experienced in Ellised. This particular storm swirled in clouds of moisture, pushing beyond the window of the carriage and gradually soaking into his coat.

They rode through a series of mounds, like coal heaps, until he felt an unpleasant stirring within. It began as if he'd eaten something bad and ended up as a major headache.

"We're getting close," Jake said. He sounded a million miles away. The carriage slowed and the guardian was now sitting upright. "The hounds won't take us any further."

Rogan frowned. "Can't blame them, if they're feeling how I'm feeling."

His boots sank partially into the ground as he alighted. Drifts of fine rain swept by, partially obscuring the surrounding terrain. He kept the umbrella furled and pulled up his hood, following Jake who was already striding up a steep incline.

He felt something pulling on his heart while an invisible foe stabbed at the scar on his upper chest, and he was seriously considering he might not make it to the top when the crest of the hill arrived and the view beyond silenced all the noise.

Directly ahead, the ground fell away in an easy descent that eventually met another great body of water. A number of wooden jetties hovered like rotten fangs, partially collapsed and stretching out beyond the shore. Shallow waves rolled toward a pebbled beach. The accompanying sound became the soft inhale and exhale of a mighty, invisible giant. These were the details he absorbed while summoning the courage to look at what hovered in the air directly above the shoreline.

Jake was setting off down the incline. "It's grown larger," he said. "I feared as much."

Rogan stayed put, enabling him to get a better look and maintain what he considered a respectable distance. From his point of view it seemed as if a horizontal cut had been slashed in the air above the shoreline, and the more he stared at it, the more he felt the pulse of the inky blackness that lay beyond the rent, slithering and sliding until it fell in narrow channels and spread out among the pebbles.

Jake's descent offered him some scale. The man had reached the base of the hill and was walking across a flat plane of rock that preceded the beach. He looked tiny against the horizontal rent and its ever-growing pool of darkness. It was the Void, and it seemed fully determined to take up residence on this tattered, forlorn shore.

Reluctantly, he set off down the hill toward his companion. They were two curious crows, their coats flapping in the breeze, about to pay homage to a phenomenon that could swallow them both, and for a long moment they stood before it in silence.

"Do the others know about this?" Rogan asked eventually.

"The Sisters, naturally. I made sure Jerrad listened to me. As for the other guardians..." He trailed off.

"We should fix this before it gets too big, and before it starts a panic—"

"No one comes here, therefore no one knows."

"Except the people who work here, and I'm betting they'll have stories to tell the folks back in the

Quadrants."

"No one leaves Athed, Rogan."

"What?" He stared, incredulous. "The vessel we arrived on. You think word won't get to the sailors? You think they won't talk?"

"This isn't—"

"Oh, come on, we've already been through this. People talk. It's what we do."

A short distance away, a collection of debris rested on the pebbles; an anomaly on an otherwise pristine shore. Quickly, he approached and discovered a small pile of pink fruit alongside a shallow bowl that contained a charred piece of wood. The bowl's interior was coated with soot. He picked up one of the fruits. It felt firm and fresh, a precious consumable in a gray place such as this.

Examining the arrangement he saw certain stones, larger than the others, had been placed in a circle around the fruit and bowl. It was barely noticeable, but a distinction nonetheless. He took the fruit back to Jake who turned it over in his fingers.

"Washed ashore?"

Rogan hesitated, abruptly unsure of what to say. Would the shrine's creator get into trouble? The subsequent look on Jake's face told him it was too late to remain silent on the matter.

His companion walked to the shrine and picked up the bowl. "Why would you wish to hide your thoughts from me?"

"Maybe I dislike the idea of people getting killed because I chose to express an idea."

"And yet your thoughts were loud and clear."

"I keep forgetting."

Jake replaced the bowl and stared out across the water. He seemed to be struggling to make sense of it all.

"Your dragons are revered, yes?"

"Yes."

"And yet there's no dragon, here. Perhaps they needed something else."

"The Sisters."

"Or the Void."

Jake laughed. "No. You're overthinking this."

"Am I?" He hadn't considered the Sisters. Maybe Jake was right. Was he simply thinking the worst because that's what he did? The thought accompanied him as he and Jake stepped back once more to take in the size of the rent splitting the air above their heads.

"Okay, so what do we do? I'm assuming other places aren't similarly afflicted?"

"No, this is the only one."

"If it succeeds in taking Athed, it'll try for the others."

"I fear so, yes."

"Then we have to fix this." He gestured to the hillside behind them before switching to English. "Christ, no wonder Draken doesn't want to come home. We need to fix *all* of this."

For a moment he thought he'd broken through, that Jake's mood had shifted to something more positive, more present, but it didn't last.

He tried again. "I thought this was what you guys did. We go talk to your cousins, come up with a plan—"

"And like I keep telling you, this is not your world."

"But—"

"Enough. I must think on this."

After a growl of frustration, Rogan kept silent. They were going around in circles and until he could find a way into his companion's stubborn skull, further discussion was pointless.

Something else was bugging him as they retreated up the hill, but it wasn't until they were descending its other side toward the carriage that he realized what it was.

Out there, at the shoreline, faced with insurmountable terror, he'd felt just fine. Walking back and forth, collecting pieces of fruit and jabbering about this and that with Jake who, despite his fearsome role as guardian, had seemed unusually wary.

Naturally, Jake had been reading his thoughts, and when they were aboard the carriage, "Your reaction back there was interesting."

"Did you expect me to beg for mercy?"

The other man smiled. "Perhaps."

"After everything you've put me through, maybe I just don't care, any more."

"Or you felt, how is the saying, right at home?"

"I wouldn't go that far. And while we're discussing my mental fortitude, are you ever going to tell me what happened on the boat?"

Jake shrugged. "I didn't want you to confront the Void while you were unsettled."

I don't think we're going to like this, said the snake.

"What happened?"

"We were paid a visit by Kerross," and when Rogan looked baffled," My sister, the Mother of the Deep."

Rogan sat back in the carriage as if he'd been pushed. The great eye, rolling to the surface of the water. "What did she want?"

"I'm not sure. The fact that she appeared is surprising, although her rare sightings have always taken place on the journey to Athed."

"Maybe it takes us close. It felt different to the other places."

Jake nodded and regressed into silence, once more.

"So, what happened? Don't leave me hanging."

"What do you remember?"

"I was looking into the water. I saw an eye— enormous, like a whale—I thought I was dreaming, except when I woke up I was soaked."

"Hmmm."

"And how about you? Did she say anything? Like

hey bro', how ya doin'?" Once again he'd slipped into English in an effort to normalize the experience. Forget the Void, this latter conversation was beginning to frighten him and he had no idea why.

"I don't know what it means, but you need to calm yourself. You survived. That, in itself, should be enough."

Rogan rubbed the bridge of his nose. The headache and nausea were still rolling through him and he figured he'd be glad when they were back aboard the ship and heading home. Until Jake informed him they were taking a detour.

"It's your fault," the man said when he complained. "What you said on the beach, about reverence, I need your observations."

So, he was listening.

Son of a bitch doesn't miss a trick, snake.

The weather was improving, the drifting curtains of rain had all but disappeared, and as they traveled through the streets Rogan had the opportunity to examine more of the architecture. He could see elaborate but damaged lintels and columns adorning some of the doorways, while others showed signs of having been stripped bare of all decoration.

This whole place has been cannibalized, he thought. Used by the others to better their cities, and once again he was back to thinking how human this was, despite Jake's emphatic denials. Elsewhere, he saw collapsed roofs and rubble where walls should be. "Is some of this down to the lack of a stormkeeper?"

"Yes, although Athed is close enough to benefit from the others' efforts."

His comment made Rogan long for another map so he could see where everything fit together. Maybe his new entourage in Ellised would help. Otherwise, it was hard keeping track.

The carriage drew to a halt. "Take off your overcoat," Jake instructed, "and ensure your medal of office is visible."

"And the umbrella?"

"Leave it."

They alighted onto a cobbled square surrounded by a number of buildings that looked in better shape than the rest. There were no sparkling rooftops, but no one had absconded with the decorative masonry and the pavement was swept clean and free of rubble.

He straightened his collar as a small group of plainly-dressed people approached. He could see Jake was standing tall and he did likewise. The group was made up entirely of women. They varied in age, and it wasn't the eldest who verbally greeted them after a sweeping bow. Rogan saw her emissary medal glinting in the light as she rose.

"Excellency Jackal." Her voice was deep and warm, her hair, like the other women, was tucked beneath a plain blue shawl that fell over her shoulders. "It is good to see you."

"Emissary Benar. This is Rogan Moore, the Nembraean emissary."

"Nembrae?" The women regarded one another in astonishment.

Rogan inclined his head and paid attention to their faces. They reminded him of a group of nuns, here to greet the local bishop, and once again the shrine and suggestions of worship arrived at the forefront of his thoughts. But worship of whom?

Pushing his conjecture aside he followed Jake as they were led inside a large building that bore a domed roof. The interior took his breath away. The walls were covered in murals of legendary creatures—dragons and sea monsters—while in the background were illustrations of land and coastlines. Was this the map he was looking for?

Overtaking Jake, he strode into the center of the room and spun around in an attempt to take it all in. Directly above his head the dome was composed of small glass panels stained blue and green. Light falling through them offered the suggestion he was standing inside an enormous aquarium.

He laughed softly. "No one would dare desecrate this." A moment later he realized everyone was staring, while Jake's expression carried the usual strained patience. "Sorry," he added.

"Are you here to witness the Void?" Benar said.

The guardian nodded. "Yes, along with other business. I would like one of you to familiarize Rogan with our immediate surroundings."

A woman who'd been giving him a thorough once over approached. "I am Cianne, Emissary. I can show you what you'd like to see." She looked older than Benar, with deep brown eyes and wisps of gray hair escaping her shawl, and the more Rogan paid attention the more he realized her perception was better than most. Not like Reave, but there was enough to suggest she could see beyond his highfalutin, black-clad façade well enough.

This should be interesting, said the snake.

Rogan agreed. He was itching to take a look around.

Jake raised an eyebrow as they separated. Don't get into any trouble, it meant. *As if.*

As soon as they were out of hearing range of the others, Cianne asked, "May I be bold?"

"Always."

"Were you appointed because you're a seer? We hear terrible stories of Nembrae."

"I was appointed because I had met Draken."

The woman gasped and her piercing stare returned.

"I thought we were being bold?"

"And I'm detecting no lies." She pulled her garments close about herself. "He left us before my great-grandmother was born. Now, what would you like to see?"

"Are we close to where his palace used to be?"

"Close? We're inside it. That room back there, the one that captured your spirit, I believe it was his place of contemplation."

"It's beautiful." He remembered Draken's house in Laurel Canyon and the mural on the wall. There was no physical comparison in terms of scale and artistry, but did it represent a taste of home? "I'm hoping what I see here will give me a better understanding of him."

Cianne beckoned. "Come then. I'll do my best to show you."

They took a left turn and were met by a cold breeze. The door ahead of them was closed but badly fitted, allowing the weather to make itself felt. Rogan wished Jake hadn't insisted he remove his overcoat.

As his companion gripped the latch he spied movement and saw a young woman and a child huddled against the wall. They were barely evident. Flaking paint shone through their clothing and he struggled to decipher the expression on their faces. Not knowing what else to do, he inclined his head.

Cianne was watching him like a hawk. "Wraiths. We'll see plenty of them on our journey." She pushed open the door. Immediately, light spilled in, obliterating his view of them.

Outside, a wide, unpaved rectangle was bordered on either side by tall columns covered in vines. The layout suggested there had once been a roof, he supposed a paved floor, too, but both seemed long gone.

He stood for a moment and absorbed the scene. Here and there he spied other movement—a man walking among the columns to his left; a woman, her head covered like his companion, carrying a basket across the rectangle. Both stopped when they saw him, the scenery behind them evident in their faces and garments.

"They're used to the sight of me," Cianne explained. "But you have taken them by surprise."

"I'm sorry." It felt like an intrusion, walking among them like this.

Rain was drifting forth once more and Cianne led him quickly across the rectangle and beneath the eaves of another building, this one also possessing a domed roof.

A man opened a door as they arrived, and on seeing Rogan's medal of office he bowed low.

At least this one is alive, said the snake.

Beyond the threshold lay a chamber twice the size of the first. Alas, some of the glass panes in the roof were smashed and water had entered from above, partially ruining the tiled floor and creating a pool at its center.

There were no murals on this occasion. Instead, walls were clad with shelving, some of it now warped or collapsed. The shelves were separated at intervals by a number of ornate plinths which currently bore nothing on their upper surfaces.

"A library?" he asked, approaching the pool.

Cianne stopped whispering to the man who'd accompanied them. "Yes. I believe all records now reside in the palace cellars in Ellised."

"Yeah, I bet they do," he muttered. Did Draken know what had happened here? If so, Rogan was betting the dragon's hide was well and truly chapped over it. "How much more is there?"

She beckoned. "This way."

Leaving the man behind, they skirted the pool, left the chamber, and arrived at a balcony that looked out over the city and a sullen expanse of water.

Cianne pointed. "The flat patch of land bordered by the wall used to contain His Excellency's private quarters. Most of the wraiths gather over there, I'm not sure why."

"Is this the extent of it?" He frowned when she nodded. Taking in what he'd seen thus far, Draken's palace would occupy a quarter of Gherem's equivalent at Nefhered, and would represent an even smaller fraction of Jerrad's massive domicile.

He remembered what Draken said when they'd discussed Palladium's potential destruction. *Maybe it's time.* He was beginning to understand, now. The dragon wouldn't care if this entire dimension burned to the ground. Or would he?

"Thank you for letting me see this," he said as they returned through the partial ruin.

"Did it help you understand?"

"I'm not sure. How was Draken regarded by his people?"

Cianne appeared confused. "I don't understand."

"Loved? Hated? Somewhere in between?"

"Draken just is."

He tried a different approach. "I've been told he should have accepted death in order to make way for someone stronger, someone new."

"We have scant histories on the matter, although some have said Draken is the strongest of them all."

"I heard he was unique." He smiled in an effort to put her at ease. Only one thing left to discuss, the anomaly represented by the Void, currently an ever-encroaching presence on the shoreline, and Cianne hadn't mentioned it once. "We should talk about what's happening at the coast. You don't seem afraid."

"Neither do you."

He barked out a laugh. "I used to be."

Cianne was regarding him warily. "Your connection with your guardian is strong. As for why he would choose so powerful a seer, one who can see the darkness in his heart—" She looked away.

"Look, we're here to help. There has to be a way of shutting it down."

"And yet it remains open and some have already been lost."

"What do you mean, lost?"

"I have said too much."

Rogan struggled with what he was hearing. "You mean dead? How many?"

"I don't know. And neither do I know if they're dead." Her accusatory tone suggested she knew exactly, but the number was now lying behind a wall of mistrust.

Looking out into the city he asked, "When did it begin? When did the rent appear?"

"Six quadrants, maybe a little longer."

"And there are no guardians based here?"

He frowned as she shook her head. Someone of Jake's or Telenth's caliber would have fixed this in its early stages for sure. What he continued to struggle with, was how none of them had known, and if they had, why hadn't they done something about it?

He felt helpless alongside her, knowing she'd see through every platitude, and he was grateful when he became aware of Jake tugging at his thoughts.

They found Jackal and Emissary Benar where they'd left them. Jake appeared gloomy, as if his conversation had traveled along similar lines, and after saying their goodbyes, they were soon back aboard the carriage and Rogan was once more bundled up in his overcoat in an effort to escape the surrounding chill.

"How did you get on with Benar?"

"She's hiding something."

"Did she tell you people were being lost in the rent?"

"Your guide told you this?"

"Yes. Something about not being sure if they'd died was disturbing too."

"There's strangeness at work, here."

"I don't think it's strange at all. We shouldn't underestimate the Void's allure. I remember what Reave told me. She was totally smitten."

"Meaning, we're back to that little shrine on the beach?"

"I don't know, Jake. I know so little about this place and you're not exactly Chatty Cathy on the subject."

"Chatty Cath—?"

"Never mind."

They were at the dock and about to climb out of the carriage when he came up with an idea. "I'd like to pay Tiber a visit, in the Quadrants."

"The slave traders? They could have connections in Athed."

"Perhaps, but more to the point, Tiber is dead and I saw a number of ghosts haunting Draken's old palace. Maybe they know some things." *Things you're reluctant to tell me.*

And if he refuses? asked the snake. *You should have kept it quiet and gone there on the down low.*

But there were already too many secrets. No point

in imploring Jake to share the truth if he, too, was skulking around.

His companion said nothing as they left the carriage. Looking out across the water, Rogan could see a few distant rays of light trying to break through the mist.

They boarded a vessel similar to the last. Two solemn men wearing long overcoats stood ready on the quayside to cast off the ropes, and just the act of disconnecting physically from this unhallowed ground unlocked a tense feeling that had been building in his gut ever since they'd landed.

"Let me think on it," Jake told him before disappearing below deck.

The murky silhouette of Athed's harbor was soon swallowed by fog as they headed out. He found a spot close to the mast, hunkered down, and the crew very kindly brought him blankets and food.

Thoughts of the earlier journey churned in his innards as they sailed through the gloom. Had they really encountered the mighty Kerross, Mother of the Deep? Was she aware of the situation on Athed? Had she just popped up for a look-see or did she have something else in mind? His imagination put together all manner of suggestions.

A cry from the lookout made him pay attention. A shift in air pressure made his ears pop while his fingers gripped nearby coils of rope. After a nausea-inducing lurch, up or down, he had no clue, he noticed the mist was breaking over the water, and he saw the faint outline of Ellised's harbor. Jake arrived from below, soon after.

"That was a much shorter journey."

"Yes. And I think a conversation with the wraith is a good idea."

Rogan raised an eyebrow, but said nothing more. Together they watched their approach to the harbor. He breathed deep, glad to get Athed out of his system, and when he alighted onto the dock he felt a spring in his step, borne of blissful relief.

At the palace they separated. Jake mentioned something about a meeting with Jerrad and seemed happy to leave him to his own devices. Thinking no more about it, he collected his umbrella and set off. It was easy enough to acquire passage, in fact he had the offer of two ships that were heading for the Quadrants, but on recognizing the captain from his first ever journey the choice became easy.

"Glad to have you aboard, Emissary, and may our voyage be an easy one."

Once again, the journey seemed faster than usual, as if some mysterious force wanted him in the Quadrants at all speed, and as they approached the dock he was startled when Tiber appeared abruptly alongside him at the rail.

"I implore you, do not leave this vessel."

Rogan frowned. There'd been no preamble, no hey it's good to see you, and Tiber looked uncharacteristically scared.

He became aware of an aura, not unlike Jake's, one that quickly intensified as he spotted two tall figures standing with a group of tough-looking men. He gestured toward his medallion. "Don't worry. They won't start anything while this is hanging around my neck."

"Please, Rogan, don't do this."

This wasn't the Tiber he knew, and once more he regarded the dock where two Khir'gham Guardians of the Void waited. He recognized Longhair, and the other one whose name he hadn't been given during the meeting at Jake's house.

"I wanted you to come with me to Athed," he whispered. "We have a problem to solve, and the wraiths there might have some answers."

"Athed? But—"

"No matter. Make yourself scarce and let me handle this."

The ship was edging toward the quay and the crew were throwing out the necessary ropes. Rogan removed his overcoat, gripped his umbrella and stood tall. His medal hung like a two-ton rock around his neck. What the hell did these bastards want?

A quick glance informed him Tiber had disappeared. Nothing else to be done now except bluff it out while he figured out what was going on. His steps were nimble, and there was an affable smile on his face as he walked the narrow gangway. There'd be no bow, either. Screw that. "Gentlemen," he began, "to what do I owe the pleasure?"

8

BROWN

The confidence underpinning Brown's assurances to Mrs. Orsen was like thin ice atop a deep, treacherous pond. He wished fervently that Rogan would rejoin them so they could talk about Draken's demands. Unfortunately, one day led to another, and another, and there was no sign of the younger caretaker. Caroline Aldred was becoming restless, too. Rogan had, after all, promised to fix her yard.

Feeling somewhat useless, Brown hung out in his usual spot by the Rothe house gate while others paid him an occasional visit with snippets of information on Draken that didn't really amount to much, until finally the house's irascible neighbor summoned him to her ivy-smothered fence.

"I'm sorry, Ma'am," he began. "I don't know where he is."

"Come," she said, and disappeared beyond the fence.

With no other choice, Brown did as he was told, climbing over the fence and joining her in the partially tidied front yard. The area had seen the benefit of a short, sharp rainstorm the previous evening leaving an array of shallow pools and puddles, and it was over one of them she was currently crouched.

"Tell me what you see," she said, beckoning impatiently.

With trepidation, he advanced. She required him to stare into a pool of water? He was baffled until he caught a glimpse of other puddles as he passed by. It seemed to him they were not composed of rainwater at all, and instead appeared like holes in the ground that led elsewhere. Grey leaves swaying in one of them, and within another lay a sky the color of vermilion decorated with pale clouds.

"Here," she hissed. "Stop dilly-dallying. My power isn't endless."

Quickly, after stepping over what looked like a dizzying canyon whose depths were full of twinkling stars, he arrived at her side. Before them an image of a maelstrom. Dark clouds swirled, folding within themselves. The effect rendered him nauseous. "What is it?"

"It's Rogan."

He absorbed her expression of consternation as she regarded the pool of water. "Does this mean he's in trouble?"

"Ha," she barked. "I would say so, wouldn't you?"

"He's in Palladium. He followed Jake—"

"Would that *creature* deliberately do him harm?"

"It's an odd relationship, but I don't think he'd hurt him without cause."

"There is cause now, it seems. Unless they are both under threat."

"But what can we do? We can't get down there—"

"We know someone who can."

Brown took a guess. "Reave?"

"It's a risk we'll have to take."

He took a step back from the swirling pool. Any more and he'd pitch forward and be lost. "And if she refuses?"

Caroline Aldred stood and wiped her hands vigorously, as if she'd gotten them dirty while observing the dizzying swirl. "I'll give you the means to free her. Tell her to ruminate on her surroundings, and ask if she wishes to remain there. I'm sure it will be enough."

She went on to tell him where Reave was and how to set her free. Had he been a cartoon, the revelation would have made his eyes pop out and his ghostly jaw drop to the floor.

He asked Mrs. Orsen to help him, not trusting himself to perform the task on his own. "Flos tenebrarum, nosce te ipsum. I have no idea what it means."

His companion regarded him with dismay. "Nosce te ipsum is easy enough. It means know thyself, and flos means flower I seem to remember. What happens when we tell her this?"

Brown shrugged. "I have no idea, other than it's supposed to snap her out of it and allow her to help us."

"We'd better do it while it's daylight, then. Something tells me it'll be more difficult at night."

The journey involved a couple of ghostly hops across the Southern California terrain. Brown knew the whereabouts of Chino airport which lay a few miles south west of the Rothe house, and after a quick reconnoiter they were soon standing outside the gates of the California Department of Corrections and Rehabilitation's California Institute for Women that lay directly south of the tiny airport.

"Now comes the difficult part," said Orsen, as always, stating the obvious. "Can you remember what she looks like?"

"Of course I can." Although he mused it was doubtful she'd look like the chic woman he'd first encountered.

It turned out they were in luck. One section of the prison grounds held a quadrangle of turned earth and a group of inmates were out there digging, hoeing, and weeding under the supervision of a number of correctional officers.

Brown approached a slight woman in her thirties, dark hair tied back, dressed in baggy scrubs and a white T-shirt. She was poking at the hard ground with a hoe and seemed determined on her task.

For a moment he baulked, wondering if he'd gotten it wrong and was about to utter Latin to someone who couldn't even see him. But there was no need to worry, for she looked up, startled, as they arrived.

"Well, at least she's seen us." Orsen was taking in their surroundings. "What a terrible place. All this hot sun, and I smell cow dung."

Brown ignored her and focused on the female prisoner. This had to be Reave. It had to be. "We didn't mean to startle you," he began, and while she stood blinking and uncomprehending he told her about the mission and what might happen if she refused.

At one point he paused for a habitual but unnecessary breath, during which Mrs. Orsen took the bull by the horns and offered up the Latin phrase. Annoyed, he turned on her. "Why did you do that? I wasn't ready."

"It wasn't registering. Didn't you see her face—?"

"Actually, it was."

The words arrived softly, and when Brown renewed his attention he saw the woman's posture and facial expression had been transformed.

"Well, shit." Reave was leaning on her hoe and looking around, utterly bemused. Thankfully, no one else in the immediate area had noticed. "Did that nasty old witch's protections extend to you two?"

"Yes," Brown lied, far too quickly to be convincing.

"Very well, then. Off you go."

He pulled the speechless Mrs. Orsen away from the scene. He didn't want to go straight back to the house. Instead, he brought them to a stretch of grass alongside the taxiway at Chino airport, where a red and white Cessna was chugging toward the runway.

"That was astonishing." Orsen appeared stunned. "The power she has. How on earth did Aldred subdue her?"

"I don't know. I also don't know how she managed to be there without the authorities noticing they'd gotten an extra prisoner."

"I'm in awe. That's two *very* powerful women." Orsen's face had grown wistful, like a schoolgirl suddenly acquiring a crush on two of her teachers.

He was about to tell her to knock it off, and warn her why he'd lied about Caroline's protection. The other ghosts' warnings were ringing in his ears, about how she might use their energy. But before he could, the ground dipped and momentarily disappeared. Brilliant blue sky immediately faded to gray.

When he came to, or at least when his surroundings did, he felt severely winded as if he'd been kicked resoundingly in the stomach. He felt diminished. Was this how the others had felt? As for Mrs. Orsen, there was no sign of her at all.

Looking south across the airstrip he stared in fear and wonder. "What did you do, Reave? What did you just do?"

9

ROGAN

He tried being polite, he tried threats, he tried pleading. Alas, none of it worked, and after resorting to physical means in order to protect himself he now had a growing lump above his left eye after a short and unsuccessful skirmish.

At least he'd managed to land a spectacular blow on the jaw of Longhair who'd gone sprawling. But it was to no avail. They'd come prepared with half a dozen men, some of whom he hoped were similarly banged up, and now he was back on a boat, tied up like a Thanksgiving turkey and stowed below deck.

No one had said where they were going but he'd

put money on them arriving in Athed at some point. He hoped Tiber had managed to escape. For a wraith it shouldn't have mattered, but after the business with Reave's worm and the guardians' consequent study of it, he suspected it now mattered quite a bit.

As for the protection offered by his status, it appeared useless, and however much he tried to figure out why, nothing made sense until he considered Jake's behavior earlier in the day, and that's when his mood really tanked.

Did you tell them where I was, Jake? Did you tell them?

Don't go there, said the snake. *Let's focus on escape?*

The creature had a point, but thus far he'd been unable to loosen his bonds. He continued pulling at the ropes tying his wrists. They refused to give, and all he did was rub the flesh raw until it really hurt. He'd already established that he'd been dumped in the ship's hold. It was completely dark, and other than the soft undulation of the ship through the water, his imagination would have convinced him he'd been swallowed by the Void.

Okay, wiseass, now what?

He thought about Reave and how she would react in this situation. That she'd managed to survive in the clutches of these treacherous bastards, suggested there'd be a way out, and a fanciful notion arrived, involving the conjuring of a hellish creature that would gnaw through his bonds and allow him to ride on its back to the land of escape and vengeance.

The whole idea was ridiculous. Nonetheless, it lit a fire in him, and by the time his captors had lifted the hatch, his thoughts had shifted from a physical means of escape to possibilities that were entirely alien in nature.

He closed his eyes and shut out the noise. Vaguely, he was aware of a discussion about him as they carried him off the ship and dumped him aboard a carriage.

"—Jackal's fault lies in becoming too enamored—"

Rogan kept his face impassive. Enamored? Jake had thrown him to the wolves. And assuming he'd gotten this right they were headed right back to the shoreline where the abyss waited. Naturally, there was a chance he was mistaken. He hadn't opened his eyes once on leaving the ship. He hadn't trusted himself. But there was no mistaking the damp air and the moody silence, or the soft footfalls of the sullen shoremen. The prevailing atmosphere danced behind his eyes, offering up visions of impending doom.

Lulled by his apparent dormancy his captors left him alone, maybe because they thought capitulation was normal for someone like him.

Jake didn't advise them well, offered the snake.

He also didn't object to me contacting Tiber, suggesting he's playing a game of his own, but I'm still pissed.

All the times I've told you to run—

Shut up.

A headache and a weird, hollow feeling in his chest told him they were close. In the meantime, he'd been searching within himself, looking for particles of the Void left behind after previous battles. He remembered when he'd wanted it all out. All of it. Only to acknowledge later that tiny pieces still remained, embedded in his heart and lungs, wisps of it seeking sanctuary among his other organs. Was his reluctance to purge it entirely mere carelessness, or because he feared without it he'd fall apart? It was hard coming to terms that he was a different man.

As the carriage drew to a halt and he was dragged stumbling over the rise it became pointless to remain blind any longer. Looking down at the shore he saw other people had gathered, not the entire town, but certainly more than he'd seen on his last visit. They were standing in a single line along the shore, their long coats billowing in the turbulence from the rent, and every face was turned toward him.

Closer still and he gasped in horror. Only half of those standing at the shore were alive. Every alternate figure was a wraith, as if the townsfolk had each brought a dead relative along. But why?

Clarity arrived when he was hauled to the water's edge and was able to see the expression on the wraiths' faces. Dread, fear. He was their herald of doom and they were here to be used.

He regarded the Void, still a sickly, gaping wound, before observing his Khir'gham captors who had no intention of fixing it. They'd been using it to experiment. They wanted to recreate Reave's monsters, and here was Rogan to show them how. The aura of expectancy growing at the water's edge was making his teeth ache. He spotted Emissary Benar among the living, her anticipation dark and hungry across her face.

Longhair was smiling. "Jackal told us you might not agree, and yet, with your skills we would be better equipped to protect our land. While you, in turn, could live a very rich life."

He's lying, said the snake. *This is a power grab.*

I know. Let me think.

Better make it quick.

Rogan offered up his bound hands. "I can't do anything like this."

Longhair's fellow guardian nodded to the men who'd been doing all the strong-arm stuff. A dour lot, they reminded him of the guy who'd let young Lennox loose from the line of prisoners in Tyfohwed. One of them approached, knife in hand. Rogan gave him an affable smile.

When his hands were free he took a few steps toward the waiting line at the shore. There appeared to be some connection between the living and the dead but he failed to understand what it was.

"Rest easy," he said. "I don't need you." He was

addressing the wraiths, attempting to regard each one in turn. Old men and women for the most part. He counted thirty at least, some mere shadows, others as robust as their living companions. As for their reaction, relief swept through him like a tidal wave.

Turning away, he approached the shore where the daunting rent fluttered, occasionally dropping slivers of the Void into oily pools in the shallows below. Somehow, he had to pretend he was doing what they asked while hiding his real intentions. Anger tempered his resolve and gave him courage. This was Jake's fault, and Rogan was being dangled like a baited fly.

He rolled his shoulders and raised his hands. *Nice knowing you, snake.*

Tendrils of the Void swam along veins and capillaries, meeting at his fingertips. After that he wasn't sure what would happen. He was working on an idea, backed up by belief in his capabilities, and what Jake and Reave had taught him.

When he was finally done he was soaked to the skin. Just the act of raising the Void from where it had fallen, had revealed open trenches which the water had ebulliently rushed in to fill. Waves had swept up the shore, rattling pebbles and drenching anyone standing too close.

Rogan was on his knees, laughing and delirious. His hands hurt. They hurt bad. Meanwhile, the air above him was clear of the dark menace. The rent had been sealed, and the atmosphere would have improved immeasurably were it not for the guardians' heavies, bearing down.

"You see?" He giggled as they hauled him upright. "I'm not here to make monsters. I don't know how."

One of the men punched him in the face and he fell back into the water. Longhair's colleague approached and pulled him to his feet. His touch, fingers grasping at his throat, felt cold as ice and immediately the Void within Rogan swam toward the contact. The guardian immediately gasped and let go. He stared at his hand which now appeared fragile and misshapen. Tiny specks of darkness were rising from the man's fingertips and into the air. The extremity began to collapse and dissolve.

"Touch me again and I'll kill you," Rogan said. He received another punch, heavier than the last, and this time it was lights-out.

On awakening he discovered they'd locked him in a cell crowded with wraiths. Some were standing, huddled in corners, while others were sitting cross-legged on a stone floor partially covered with sawdust, watching, waiting.

"He's awake." The announcement silenced ambient chatter and they drew so close he could no longer see the dimensions of his prison.

Sitting up, he massaged his temples. Not too heavily on the right side where that last blow had rendered him unconscious. It felt horribly tender. "How long have I been here?" Briefly, he looked up where light was coming from an overhead grate.

"A night and two full days." An old woman was sitting directly alongside him, who reached out and gently stroked his forearm. In the dappled light he saw the thin outline of a mermaid tattoo above her wrist. "Hold fast," she added before withdrawing her hand.

He had no idea what she meant by that, and was about to utter some stupid quip when he heard footsteps. Immediately, his wraith companions vanished except for the old lady and a couple of older men. Thankfully, whoever was on the approach walked by the other side of a metal-studded door, and when they'd gone most of the other wraiths returned, crowding in like sardines.

Wearily, he crawled until he could sit with his back to the wall opposite the door. He discovered a jug of water and a tall basket of stale bread. Quickly, he tucked in. His companions watched. They seemed mesmerized by his every move and he wished Tiber was here, or better still, Gregory Brown.

Don't suppose anyone has a key?" he asked, his mouth half full. The cell erupted with laughter and he considered they'd drive him mad.

"Can you see all of us?" one of the men asked.

"I'm not sure. Most of you, I guess?"

"His words arrive in the wrong order." More laughter.

The woman with the tattoo sensed his bewilderment. "They're happy you didn't destroy us."

Rogan frowned. "I was told people had been delivered into the rent."

"Pushed," one of the men said, his long robes billowing.

Bitterly, he recalled the small arrangement of artifacts on the shore. It was starting to make sense. It wasn't a shrine, it was a memorial. At the earlier gathering they'd been lied to. Emissary Benar—her face at the shore had carried a malevolent gleam which she had obviously hidden when they'd first met. He hadn't sensed a thing. At least he hadn't seen Cianne, his guide, in the crowd.

He thought about Jake and what he'd said, about playing around with Reave's little toy, finding out what made it tick.

Holy fuck, snake, they've been murdering people, the living and the dead.

And we shouldn't be at all surprised.

Disconsolately, he brushed his fingers against his chest, discovering the medallion of office. So much for its protection. Longhair and his cronies hadn't given it a moment's thought. Maybe, at some point, there'd be a reckoning and they'd suffer the misfortune of Jerrad's wrath. Except by the time the irascible dragon had gotten around to it, Rogan would be dead.

We'll have to figure this out on our own, said the snake.

"What are the guardians planning on doing with me?" he asked the surrounding specters.

"They're intent on destroying you, but they're not sure how."

"It's what you did," added another. "They're calling you a disrupter. Excellency Rolat still does not have the use of his hand."

"Rolat, huh? What's the name of the other?"

There was a moment of hesitation, protocol he assumed, before the old man in the flowing robes threw caution to the wind. "Excellency Quin, who isn't a Khir'gham one should cross. What he lacks in strength he more than compensates with a cold knife of resolve."

And to think, we thought him the more placid of the group, said the snake.

Yeah well, maybe we'll shove that cold knife of resolve up his ass. How about that?

"How do I get out of this cell? Any suggestions?" He watched their faces register confusion. Not one of them was displaying an ounce of guile or cunning and he considered he was doomed.

Perhaps "Touch me again and I'll kill you," was

coming on a bit strong, said the snake after a few minutes of ruminating.

I don't care. I'm sick of being pushed around.

Okay, but all they need do is leave you here until you die of thirst.

He checked his water jug, it was bone dry. The bread basket was empty, too, and already he was hungry. Rising to his feet he explored the boundaries of his cell, looking for weaknesses and finding none. He even jumped and grasped the barred grille above his head, but it was solidly embedded in the ceiling and didn't offer up the slightest rattle. Meanwhile, his ghostly companions were watching every move and he felt like a fool.

Something caught his eye. It was the tattoo on the arm of the old woman and it inspired an idea. He beckoned. "May I ask your name? Mine is Rogan."

Whispers rose in the cell like an eerie wind. "That goes for all of you, if you wish it. My name is Rogan."

The old woman stepped forward. "My name is Heldi."

He held up his hand for a moment as the others approached with their own introductions. "I need you to find Cianne," he said. "Tell her I need help. Are you able to do that? Tell her Iveryn rescued me, once."

Immediately, the ghost winked out of sight and he was left with a crowd of her companions, eager to give him their names. He absorbed what he could, and afterward they seemed content to settle in silence while he ruminated over his predicament.

With nothing better to do he went back to examining his hands. The realization of what he'd done to the guardian Rolat was finally sinking in, and the more he considered the implications the more they worried him. Did Jake know about this? Is that why he was acting weird? The possibility that Rogan could take apart Jake and his treacherous cousins seemed ridiculous, and yet— no wonder they had him locked up.

So, now what? Did he wait and hope Cianne would contact Iveryn?

Quit that. We need to find a way out.

He pressed his fingertips together, feeling some resistance. Turning to his fellow inmates he said "I'm about to try something and I think it's best if you leave."

He held up his hands in order to demonstrate and it didn't take them long to get the message. The cell dimensions grew exponentially as, one by one, they winked out of sight.

Staring at the grate above his head, he remembered how easy it was when Longhair—Quin— and his buddies had dragged him to the shore. There, he'd known exactly what he was going to do, whereas now...

Obviously, his subconscious had it down but wasn't for sharing. Same with wrangling Jake's construct. He'd simply dealt with it and not taken explanatory notes afterwards.

However, a short while later, he had some luck. Tiny capillaries of inky blackness extended from his fingertips, they stretched out and threaded through the grate. Giddy with success, he pulled. Immediately, his construct collapsed. He was about to try again when he saw shadows moving above. Moments later, a face appeared at the bars.

"Still alive, Rogan?"

In shock, he stared, open-mouthed.

"It's okay, you can thank me later."

"Reave? How the—?"

"Shh, let me focus."

"Wait—" He gasped, feeling a sharp tug inside his chest. He managed two steps back before the grate dropped with a loud clatter on the cell floor.

A hand extended. "Quickly. Before they come running."

As soon as her fingers locked onto his hand the pulling sensation in his chest expanded to his shoulders and lungs. Somehow, she was able to lift him quite easily until they were both crouched on the cobbled floor of a narrow corridor barely illuminated with intermittent skylights.

Rogan coughed. "I thought you were gonna turn me inside out."

She wasn't listening. Instead, she was staring at the medallion hanging around his neck. "Huh," was all she said before rising quickly to her feet. She offered him a hand once more which he took in order to steady his shaking limbs. "Sorry, there were none of the dead around so I had to use the living. Come on, we need to get out of here."

He took in his surroundings. Light from outside suggested it was daytime. A gentle patter suggested rain.

"This way." Reave set off immediately to their right.

Rogan followed, still struggling to reacquire his stamina. When they paused by a narrow doorway he couldn't help noticing CORRECTIONAL FACILITY emblazoned on the back of her ill-fitting sweatshirt, and he was still puzzling it out when they rounded the corner and stepped out in the open.

Rain drifted like curtains of gauze across a large quadrangle. Rogan shivered, wishing he still had his overcoat. "Who sent you? I'm guessing you didn't volunteer."

"Nope, and you might not believe me when I tell you."

"Not Draken, surely."

"Try your next door neighbor."

"But we don't—you mean Mrs. Aldred?" Her beloved garden. Oh, boy, was he in trouble, now.

"Yes, and I have a major bone to pick with that witch."

He stared at her in dismay. "Look, I can't just disappear. Not until I know what's going on."

"Is this about Jackal?"

"Maybe it's about Rolat and Quin."

"Jesus, Rogan, you're keeping dangerous company."

"No shit. Look, come with me."

"No. Jackal will kill me on sight."

"He won't if I ask him not to. How do we get out of here."

She pointed. "Lower side of the palace. There's a shortcut into town and the docks."

They made a dash for it. In the meantime Rogan attempted to reach Jake but it was useless. He felt cast off, popped out of gear. He had no sense of the guardian whatsoever.

They encountered no one as they dashed along narrow cobbled streets that tilted toward the harbor. Not even the wraiths, which made the city appear more abandoned and forlorn than ever. When they reached the base of the hill, he slowed considerably, still gasping for breath. "Give me a second."

Reave grinned. "Not a chance, and I'm sorry, but this is going to hurt."

He gasped and dropped to his knees. Directly before him, an ugly slit of darkness appeared, its edges fluttering, seeking to expand. He felt a hand on his shoulder, grasping and pulling. He lost his balance and tumbled forward, landing face first on the pavement outside the Rothe house.

"Oww…"

Reave was alongside him, gasping for air. "*That* was expensive. Now, get inside the house and call me an Uber."

"Just give me—"

"Now. I don't care if you have to crawl."

Wearily, he rose and approached the gate. His nose was dripping blood after landing so hard. Grimes and Mrs. Harris were already running down the path. He saw Harris's face assume an angry glare as she recognized who was sitting across the street, cross-legged, in the act of removing her incriminating sweatshirt.

"Mr. Moore—"

"I'll explain later. Right now, I need an Uber."

"A what?" asked Grimes.

They had to get Lennox, who download the necessary App on someone's phone.

Harris remained steadfastly hostile. "She's not coming in for a cup of tea, I can tell you that."

Rogan was near collapse and made it as far as the concrete steps before he crumbled. Dr. Halberd took a seat alongside him. "Anything broken? There's blood on your face."

"I'm just tired, but I need to get back there."

"Not like this, Mr. Moore. I think a period of rest is in order. Is she about to give us any trouble?" He nodded toward the gate.

"I don't think so." He leaned forward. "And I'll be fine if I just sit here for a while."

When he came to it was nightfall, his cottage was in semi-darkness and the curtains were open, enabling him to see light spilling from the main house. There was also someone sitting in the chair usually occupied by Mrs. Harris when she was nursing him back to health, but on this occasion it wasn't Mrs. Harris and the accompanying aura felt sour and cloying.

"Dr. Halberd said you used the Void in order to escape." Jake was leaning back, legs outstretched, ankles crossed, hands clasped nice and easy in his lap. It was an attempt to appear nonchalant but Rogan knew better.

"Not me. Reave."

"Ah."

Silence followed, during which time his companion's sullen mood soaked beneath his skin, stirring up a cauldron of anger and anxiety. "I wanted to stay. I wanted to know what the hell was going on, but she—"

"I would have killed her on sight."

"I guess she knew that."

"I don't blame you for running."

"I didn't run." He growled, exasperated. "Rolat and Quin, did you know what they did?"

"Yes."

"Did you use me as bait?"

"The Void is an immense source of power, and having seen the possibilities, Quin in particular—"

"You used me as bait."

"Yes."

"What else aren't you telling me?"

"Rogan—"

"Hey, it was me they were beating up on that shore. I'm entitled to an explanation."

Jake closed his eyes. "The Sisters needed proof of corruption."

"Is that why Kerross gave me the once over? To see if I was up to the task?"

"Or, if you were likely to corrupt them further."

"Well, that's just great. I suppose it didn't occur to you to put in a good word?"

"When it comes to you, Kerross knows where I stand."

The conversation was proving exhausting but, stubborn as a mule, he kept it rolling. "And where *do* you stand, Jake? I thought—I thought we were becoming friends."

"They frightened you. I'm sorry."

"Sure you are, until something else happens and you use me again—"

"No. It's been decided. The Sisters have agreed on another course." Jake stood. He eclipsed the room. "I came here to say goodbye."

"What?" Rogan struggled to rise. "That's it?" He barely made it into a sitting position. Reave had used him like a car battery and completely wiped him out. Jake's silhouette loomed before him, silent, impenetrable. The man's thoughts were closed off, a callous rebuttal of everything they'd ever been through.

He sank back onto the pillows. "Fine. Go, then. Have it your way, and I don't want to see your sorry hide again." He watched the shadows shift and diminish until once again he could see lights from the main house, shining gently through the window.

Now Jake's presence ceased to be a massive rock crushing his chest he began to breathe easier and felt strength easing into his limbs. For a long moment he stared at the ceiling.

The Sisters have agreed on another course.

Rogan sat upright, and once again he was hardly able to breathe.

I came here to say goodbye.

"Wait a minute, what did you mean?" Tumbling out of bed he stubbed his toe on a leg of the chair, and cracked his elbow against the closet door while struggling to get dressed. His footsteps weaved alarmingly as he stumbled across the lawn. "Come back here! What did you mean?"

Remnants of Jake's thoughts drifted inside his head. The creature had been unable to hide them all, and by the time Rogan reached the kitchen, not only was he severely winded, he was seized with a terrible panic.

Mr. Grimes and Mrs. Harris found him crawling up the main staircase.

"What is it?" Mrs. Harris said. "Have they been fighting, again?"

"I'm assuming so." Grimes was holding Rogan's arm which had been flailing in an attempt to find some grip on the balustrade. "His Excellency swept by here a few minutes ago, all fire and brimstone."

Harris took his other arm. "Enough, Mr. Moore. You're in no state to go anywhere like this."

In the end he had to give up. He simply didn't have the strength to continue. "Don't you see?" he croaked. "They're going to kill him. They're going to destroy the guardians."

I have something that'll knock you right out.

He remembered Mrs. Harris's words from all those months ago. He'd declined at the time, and on this occasion she'd administered a hefty dose of the mysterious concoction under the pretense of offering him a cup of tea. Halfway down the cup he'd been babbling about going after Jake until his head had abruptly hit the kitchen table.

When he awoke his curtains were closed but there were cracks of daylight shining through, painting bold stripes across the wall. He rose, his head clear and his strength returned. Methodically, he showered, got dressed in jeans and a T-shirt and slipped the medallion into his pocket.

When he arrived in the kitchen Mrs. Harris was waiting, she was alone, and for a long moment they stared at one another.

"How long was I out?"

"Eight or nine hours, give or take. I made you some breakfast, and a sandwich to take with you. Make sure to see Lennox before you go," she added.

Cautiously, he slid into his usual seat while his anger at being drugged went head to head with a strong dose of common sense. There was, after all, no way he could have gone after Jake last night. Nonetheless, it was only when he was part way through a plate of bacon, sausage and toast did he become partially reconciled. "Where *is* Lennox?"

Harris was sitting at the table's opposite side, her arms folded, watching him like a hawk. "He's next door."

He put down his fork. "What?"

"Go see for yourself when you're done."

His sense of panic re-emerged. Deliberately, he finished his breakfast, placed his fork carefully across his plate, and stood.

"Mr. Moore—" she began.

He took a deep breath. "It's okay, Mrs. H., and thank you for breakfast."

Outside, a big part of him wanted to dash back to the cottage, grab some belongings and enter the tunnel, while another part of him was scared of what he might find.

He might be dead already.

Shut up, snake.

He quickened his pace and searched out Lennox, discovering Mr. Brown hovering outside the Italianate front gate. The ghost gave him an odd look as he approached. "It's good to see you. I'm sorry I wasn't there when you returned, only Reave was there and—"

"It's okay. I know what she does."

"She nearly wiped out Mrs. Orsen completely when we rescued her."

Rogan frowned, puzzled. "You'll have to bring me up to speed." He looked beyond the open gate where two figures were standing in the Italianate's front yard. "What's going on?"

"Seems young Lennox has picked up your gardening duties."

Anxiously, he entered the yard, but on the approach it seemed there was nothing to fear. Caroline Aldred looked radiant. Fleshed out, with no sign of the illness that had caused her demise, and her clothing looked as if it had been put through the laundry. She looked like Lennox's older sister.

The boy's face lit up as he arrived. "We've been going through the Park Seed catalog." He waved the thick brochure.

For a moment Rogan didn't know what to say. Lennox didn't seem frightened or overwhelmed, as if the perusal of gardening catalogs with a witch's ghost was just fine and dandy. "Everything okay?" His words stumbled forth. "Only, I have to go back there. I have to—"

"You broke his heart," Caroline announced. "I know how that feels." Her chin was raised, her eyes narrowed in judgment.

Rogan was stunned. He regarded Lennox who was looking on, uncomprehending.

An overly dramatic assumption, said the snake. *Still...*

"I have to go back." He turned and ran, passing by an astonished Mr. Brown who was now accompanied by half a dozen of his fellow spooks. He felt their eyes boring into him as he dashed toward the gate.

At the cottage he took a deep breath and attempted to get his shit together. The medallion was already in his pocket. Raincoat and umbrella had been left behind in Palladium, and thank goodness he hadn't taken his pistol. Grabbing his keys, he unlocked a nearby drawer. The weapon was lying within, alongside two spare magazines and a box of ammunition. He stared down at them for a moment before shutting the drawer and turning the key. *We shouldn't need it*, he assured the snake. *Not anymore.*

Quickly, he retrieved one of his ever-growing collection of formal coats, all the while chastising himself that he was probably too late.

Forty minutes later, part way along the tunnel that led to the Quadrants, he realized he'd forgotten to pick up Mrs. Harris's sandwich.

10

BROWN

"But we've only just rescued him. Was it all for nothing?" Mrs. Orsen was barely visible. She also looked different. Her hair was a different color and she was wearing trousers.

"I don't know what to tell you," Brown said. "But had you been here yesterday, the atmosphere was not for the faint of heart."

"Seems to me he'll get himself into hot water all over again."

Or, he might not come back at all, Brown thought.

Beyond the Italianate's front gate he could hear the voices of Lennox and Mrs. Aldred, and he remembered it wasn't all that long ago when no one had dared enter the place.

So much was changing, it was making his head spin. They had rescued Reave, at some cost, it had to be said. The woman had done as she was asked, and he'd breathed a huge sigh of relief when a gray Prius had arrived and taken her away. As for Rogan, Brown had been filled with relief at the thought of him being back home until the Khir'gham had arrived, hot on his heels, bearing a troubled aura that had been most unwelcome.

As usual, he'd hung around the gate having no clue. No doubt Reave could have offered an explanation but he didn't fancy the idea of approaching her for a chat. He was simply a source of power to her and he had no wish to end up like Mrs. Orsen or worse.

He became aware of his companions shrinking away. Lennox and Mrs. Aldred were now on the approach. The boy offered him a wave before heading up the street toward the Rothe house with the seed catalog under his arm, and when he'd gone—

"We made a terrible mistake."

Brown stared at the woman, confused. "Begging your pardon, ma'am?"

"Come." She beckoned before turning on her heel and re-entering her yard.

His ghostly companions offered him sympathetic looks and hung back, even the much reduced Mrs. Orsen, who appeared to have had enough excitement for the time being.

No choice, he followed Caroline Aldred into her front yard where she was now staring at a large mirror that had been placed flat on the ground. "Did Lennox bring this?"

She nodded. "Look."

He looked, expecting to see a reflection of the trees and sky overhead. Instead, he saw an image of swirling darkness. He could hear it, too. Whispers on the wind, faint cries amid waves hissing back and forth on a distant shore. "What does it mean?"

"We forced the Sisters' hand. We pulled threads that should not have been pulled, and now both our worlds are in danger of falling apart."

"We should have left Rogan where he was? But I thought—"

"Oh, I'm convinced we saved his life. Nonetheless, are you ready for the dark days, Mr. Brown? For they are now upon us."

Helplessly, he looked back toward the gate where a small crowd of his fellow ghosts were gathered. One or two seemed apprehensive, but most appeared eager for him to rejoin them so he could spill the beans. Oh, but they wouldn't like this. Not at all.

Knowing there was nothing else to be done, he squared his metaphorical shoulders. "Okay, ma'am, how do we fix it?"

The story continues in
Palladium's Redemption

Made in the USA
Monee, IL
04 March 2024